Come Away

Lawrence and Keane, Volume 1

Elyse Lortz

Published by Elyse Lortz, 2021.

This is a work of fiction. Similarities to real people, places, or events are entirely coincidental.

COME AWAY

First edition. May 24, 2021.

Copyright © 2021 Elyse Lortz.

ISBN: 979-8201509200

Written by Elyse Lortz.

To those lost in the Great Snow of 1947

And to the family we have, not by birth, but by choice.

Come away, oh human child!
To the waters and the wild
With a faery, hand in hand,
For the world's more full of weeping
than you can understand

W. B. Yeats

AUTHOR'S PREFACE

Often I was appalled with the idea of an author's notice. It is a singular moment when a writer must step away from the variation of the world they had so meticulously created only to examine themselves, their faults, and their part in the ink splattered upon the pages. As the story wound on; however, I felt I really had nothing to do with the two people staring at me every time I took up the pen. I was not wholly aware of the severity of this change until they snatched the instrument from my hand and continued on their merry way without so much as a breath from me. Therefore, what have I to give but an explanation.

I met Jo Lawrence sometime within the summer of 2020 when the world had ceased its spinning axis in favor of rotating in the other direction entirely. It is the only way to describe it. Jo was, I thought, the ideal of myself, the person who could live out all the adventures I so often wished to have. I had not; however, made an exception to my plan. I had not expected a meteor to pummel my manuscripts to flames encircling my feet.

Such was Professor Brendan Keane.

As with all things, he first came as an idea, then a name, then a person entirely of himself, tugging Lawrence along with him. A few months after I first began, I realized the duo were no longer characters on the page I could maneuver with the nib of my pen, but living, breathing people who were as real to me as anything I had ever known. It was then, at a single, miraculous moment, I realized this book you are holding was no longer about me. It was no longer simply a chip of my life, but a solid part of it I will never be able to shake away, just as I shall never consider Keane to be anything less than the man whose vivid breath comes between the lines.

The story you are about to read is only as much a story as you yourself allow it to be. The words are only words until you dare to make them pictures. And behind those pleasant paintings lies the door. To enter it means you shall not be what you were before it was swung open. You can no longer feign ignorance of the world set before you. It is a chance—a gamble—all of us make in our lives. So often we choose between then and now as if we really had a say in the matter.

But perhaps that is the point.

Perhaps it is better to live day to day knowing, when the worst of it occurs, we can hold our heads up high, walk into the door, and pull the pages over our head. And, when we return, we shall have been made the better for it.

Of course, I could not have come to this point without many people who have inspired and assisted me along my path. Therefore, it is with great humility that I most sincerely thank Mrs. Maureen Kovach, Mrs. Betsy Speer, Brother Ian, Mrs. O'Reilly, Mr. Gregory Boyle, and Mr. Gerber.

PROLOGUE

It is impossible to describe the year of 1947 without including this narrative now put before you. For the sake of Keane's relations and friends, I swore I would not allow this story from my hands until the last of his great breed had died off, or were immoral enough to which such publication could cause no repercussions worse than what they had already inflicted upon themselves. The former of these has permitted the manuscript to voyage from my hands to those of the general public. Though he insists I have exaggerated somewhat (an accusation I thoroughly deny), Keane has placed a copy of this novel on the bookshelf nearest his writing desk. After all, it is his story now grasped in your eager hands.

Sincerely,
Jo Lawrence

PART ONE

We don't stop playing because we grow old;
We grow old because we stop playing.
-George Bernard Shaw

CHAPTER ONE

Ebenezer Scrooge might have been a better traveling companion in that first month of 1947. Indeed, even the common "Bah, humbug" could have been far superior to the silent grumbling I had become accustomed to throughout the years. Tales are told of men returning to their long forgotten homeland joyous and eager. These two words were not only misleading to the entire human population, but a striking opposition to the stranger with whom I now traveled. Three weeks prior, I had no knowledge of the man and certainly would not have endured his presence if Mrs. McCarthy hadn't insisted. The man beside me, crumbling the edge of an unread newspaper between his fingers, was morose beyond tendency. His poetic face grew sour with every passing mile and his normally striking blue eyes froze grey and unrecognizable. I knew not this man; yet, he had been my mentor—nay, my friend—for these last several years. I knew him as I knew myself; studied him in my former youth as one does a textbook; and once regarded him as a marble pillar on whose shoulders the world revolved.

Now it seemed much too real for my liking. His natural pallor was all the more prominent against his tweed suits and the stiffness of his movements hinted injury where there was none. He ate and drank little, but spoke even less. When he did his English voice was not only clipped, but dangerously sharp. A single newspaper occupied his hands for several hours without the pages ever being turned. Through his silence, I occupied myself by laying my head against the train window to watch enormous stretches of land leap and dive. The land seemed welcoming to all who traveled it; blessing their paths toward a future destination. Yet, it was not without some trepidation when I found myself sneaking glances at my comrade's dark overcoat lying limp beside him. Or more accurately, imagining the small, stained envelope concealed in one of the pockets.

"You could have told me you had a brother." I muttered bitterly to the cold window; my hot breath fogging the glass.

"I wouldn't have thought it necessary."

"Just as you refuse to tell me the contents of his letter?" Keane made no effort to meet my gaze, but slowly folded his newspaper, sat it on top of his coat, and pushed his hat forward onto the bridge of his nose.

"Lawrence, such remarks are unworthy of you." He grumbled; killing the briefest spark of real conversation before it could breathe and take light. Again a heavy silence settled between us; it's dark hands pouring useless curiosities into my mind as the world continued to scurry across the window. It really was beautiful, even in the winter. Deep flashes of chalk cliffs courted stones of steel grey with nothing but an openness in between that gradually became towns or cities as we blazed past. Ireland. Éire. Home.

I WAS RUDELY AWAKENED by a newspaper tapping my shoulder and the general hubbub of human bodies shoving up against each other in an effort to flood from the now stationary train out onto the platform. Keane had already done up the brass buttons of his coat and waited impatiently for me to do the same. Unlike his immaculate overcoat; however, my leather jacket was worn a bit at the elbows, the patches slightly faded, and there was a small hole in the left pocket. Keane waved the porter away and gathered up his luggage, while leaving me master of my own. Whatever frustration this show of callousness might have caused fell away the moment I stepped from the train. The stench of burning coal was suddenly cleansed by the rich fragrance of frozen earth and flavored by city life. Life. Hundreds of individuals frolicking about in a dance choreographed by a lunatic. A mother balanced her attention between two small children grabbing at her heels. A gentleman argued heatedly with a porter. An old man sold roasted nuts out of a cart. A woman struggled with a mountain of luggage. And so was the world's constant motions.

    A hand on my shoulder urged me forward into the rushing rivers of a human populous so fast and powerful one would be blind not to notice. To the wonder I was to forever fall in love with; however, the professor appeared immune. He did not stop to watch the world spin but rather pressed along as if there was no use in stopping. We marched onward through the waves; him oblivious to the spray and me lapping thirstily at it's sweetness. It was not until we were settled into the arms of a taxicab did Keane's fingers release my arm to begin the familiar ritual of opening a silver cigarette case and shoving one between his lips. With each long draw his body drained of the irksome tensions which had preyed on my nerves for the entirety of our travel. Now he looked entirely different from all forms of himself I had yet seen. The slight crinkles at the edges of his eyes turned to chiseled ravines deep enough to hold all the sorrows of the world. With each home and shop we passed all energy and anger drained from him.

    When at last the cigarette was no more, Keane did not reach for another. At the instant the silver case was returned to his pocket, the taxi slowed to a stop before a row of houses; each adjacent to the next. My companion climbed out into the cold evening air, then politely waited for me to gather myself together and join him. The building before us was a simple two story house with a white wood door and three windows to the front. Smoke poured from the chimney, promising comfort as we had not seen for many an hour. As Keane reached the doorstep, all the stiffness returned and he knocked upon the pretty door with a five fingered stone.

The next few moments came as a blur of motion as I was bustled into a well lit hall filled with the rich smells of fresh bread mingling marvelously with other equally enticing foods. Every inch of the home, for indeed it was a home, was clean, polished, and loved. No surface harbored even the slightest speck of dust. No bit of the hard floor stood un scrubbed. No man on earth could find any fault in the well-kept house. And, at the heart of it all, stood a woman.

Now I shall not say she was beautiful, for indeed she was not. Her dark hair matted together in a tangle of curls and her face was constantly contorted in what might possibly have been a smile if her lips ever decided to turn upwards, rather than remain in an unbendable line. Even so, there was a glimpse of charm to her; a merriment which had quelled ever so slightly with the passing of time. She was possibly near to Keane's age, for distinctive creases crossed her face as she stretched to kiss his cheek. It was rather a strange affair, for indeed I could count the occurrences in which I saw the professor be so demonstrative on my right hand alone. So surprised was I, it took a considerable moment to realize the woman's attention had inevitably drifted to my presence. More still, she appeared pleased.

"You must be Miss Lawrence. Brendan has written to us about you many times." I made the greatest effort to smile kindly at this while glancing at Keane, who had the grace enough to avoid my gaze. It is never a comfortable thing for a stranger to know about you, and yet you know nothing of their existence. The woman must have fallen across the same conclusion and made the effort to remedy all of which the professor had failed. "I am Catherine Keane: Thomas' wife." Thomas. So that was the brother's name. In all rights it was a good name; a title telling of leadership, and yet I remained decidedly out of place as Keane and the woman casually discussed a man I had first heard of only a few weeks before.

When a stiffness began to settle in my legs and my mind turned about ways to politely interrupt the incredibly restrained reunion, the woman suggested Keane and I go upstairs and tidy ourselves up. Dinner would be ready soon enough. Keane picked up his bags, and I followed him up a short flight of creaky wooden steps, down a moderately decorated hall, and into a room which served as a meagre shelter for two beds shoved into opposite corners. The paint on the wall had most certainly seen better days, as the once white color had dimmed into a cream. Curtains of dark green hung over a single window; a pleasant contrast to the brown blankets folded at the end of each bed. I suspected, had it been spring, a vase of flowers might have been found on the side table near the door, rather than a chipped basin and matching pitcher. The largest piece of furniture in the little room was a great wardrobe, which had no doubt been of model craftsmanship when first made.

"Keane," I whispered, lest the walls be paper. "That was all very touching, but I don't believe you dragged me all the way here for a family reunion."

"I don't believe any person with a drop of Irish blood needs 'dragged', as you so eloquently put it, but would come freely to his homeland." The dryness in what might have been powerful words caused my lips to hold back the fact he himself was a born and raised Irishman, yet no joy had I seen in his face. I merely marched over to the pitcher, rolled up my sleeves, and poured a bit of water into the basin. Cold. How ironic.

KEANE LEFT ONLY A MINUTE or so later, and I hurriedly washed my hands and face of travel's grime. It was times such as this I was incredibly thankful for my short hair, as it excused me from one of the irritable binds of femininity. I did not think my clothes in need of changing; therefore, I was free to wander back down the staircase and empty hall, this time veering toward the room emitting the most clamor.

The kitchen is, I think, the most efficient place in any well built household. It is there food is cooked and shared among its members. The warm, rich smells tugged me closer to the doorway. Keane sat at the wooden table shoved against one wall while his sister-in-law pulled things from the stove with knitted squares. It was so calm, bordering domestic. The devil himself could see it and somehow be at peace. I came forward and sat in the chair to Keane's right, and, once a dish of hot soup and bread was placed before us, Catherine moved to the empty seat opposite me. A prayer was said and the meal began. It might have been one of the most informative instances of my life, had I spent the whole of my life within the boundaries of County Cork. Catherine Keane proceeded to fill the emptiness no food could fill with the knowledge old Mrs. O'Hara ("You remember; the one with a twisted back.") had died two years before, while Fiona Kellierny had married Jamie Faversham. It was an interesting conversation, constructed of forgotten people and brief answers hardly audible to the human ear. The soup was good and hearty, and the buttered bread a trophy to behold. I could have been easily satisfied on the main course alone, but a thick, creamy custard had also been made for the occasion.

At last, our hostess folded her napkin and placed it on the table before herding the small collection of dishes toward the sink. Keane too left the table, but he took up his coat, a packet of cigarettes, and went out into the cold darkness. There I was, alone once more without proper instruction to my purpose in this small house. On most any other day, I would have followed the professor's lead for fresh air, but I felt I had spent more than enough time with his silent grumbling and might as well settle myself in the company of someone not about to brood over all that the world placed before them. Therefore, I took up a dish towel and began working. It was not out of complete selflessness I volunteered to the task. Quite the opposite, for it gave me an opportunity to study the woman I had heard nothing of but had warranted Keane's heartfelt greeting. Her hands were worn from the tedium of work, but they were nimble still, even where age may have dulled their use. Her skin was wrinkled, though not terribly so, and it bore the same paleness I had so often attributed to Professor Keane. Somewhere between the separation of bowls and plates, the woman began to speak in a slow, quiet, trail of words.

"It's a shame Thomas is working late tonight, or you might have met him today. Och, but there is tomorrow, sure enough." I nodded my agreement just as the brief light of a match flashed just outside the window. There were times I wished I smoked, if just for something to do with my hands. When one smoked, they were not required to say anything, but enjoy the comfort of another person's presence. So many times I had found no interest in such things; yet my mind pressed upon it so gravely I was unable to consider anything else for a long while.

IN THE STILLNESS OF the night one finds sleep, and yet I found none. The natural rest of the human soul tossed about the day's events; smattering the night with tepid dreams of trains and taxis. Between these foggy fantasies I awoke in expectation, waiting for some strange noise, but I heard nothing but a wind snapping at the window and a deep snoring from the room's other corner. It was the latter of these I recalled most, for it disappeared sometime near midnight when I was again startled from my sleep, this time fully expecting a silence deep and sure. But no. There; there among the night's dreary silence, there among the darkness, a quiet singing wafted up the stairs. The tune was quite bereft of any true pitch and lacked a distinguishable rhythm apart from an unsteady stomp of boots. Between ribbons of words and notes beyond any range, my ears searched for the snoring I had awoken to every time before, but it was gone. It had melted away and was replaced by the blurred outline of a figure sitting on the edge of the bed trying to do up their shoes. I watched silently from my bed as Keane slipped out the door, noting there was no 'click' behind him.

In any instance, such as this, the great drive of curiosity is questioned by human comfort. My desire to fling away the covers, dress, and rush down the stairs wavered in consideration of the frozen floors and chilled air. After all the woolen blankets and soft bed were heaven to be sure. But ah, the singing was louder now and falling even further from any song known to man. The decision was made. I jumped out of the bed (wincing mildly as my bare feet met the floor). Pulling on a pair of trousers and my jacket over the pajama shirt, I stumbled barefooted into the hall. As my eyes adjusted to the light, I saw the source of my awakening halfway up the stairs.

He was not drunk, though he had most assuredly been drinking. His hair was of a silver grey which ruffled about his head and continued down his face as a beard. The most prominent feature, even more than his nose, was a set of ears jutting out from the sides of his head. They were not enormous, but they made no lack of effort to announce their presence. As the man leaned against Keane, who had made the hasty decision to remain in his pajamas, I noticed he had green eyes: strikingly green. And yet I saw a similarity in the two blue pools staring at me. How long had I known those eyes, but they were the wrong color and, more to the point, on the wrong person. At last I mustered up a voice and a smile that did not waver with exhaustion.

"Mr. Thomas Keane, I presume?"

CHAPTER TWO

Keane had gone out early the next morning, and his brother, who I now knew through brief acquaintance, was still asleep when I ventured down the stairs at half past seven. After a hearty breakfast, I fortified my pockets with a select amount of bills and slipped out into the brisk morning air. I had no premeditated direction; no wrong to right, no memory to relive. It was only by some dull sense of curiosity I ventured up and down the sparse streets taking inventory of the city in which I had been unceremoniously thrown. By no means was it large, nor was it small. There were the basics (a few shops for food, clothing, ect . . .) and a small market set aside for other produce. A school was set aside round the bend from the Keane house; seemingly insignificant against the steel mill a mile or so on. A few pubs sprang up between some of the smaller buildings, and, like the steel mill, warranted a great deal of the public's attention. Everything had its place laid out among the rocks and greenery, and the city seemed at peace with itself.

    I was aware of nature's arms enclosing the place with gaits of green and jagged cliffs staggering over the ocean. In this sense it was very much like Devon. Even in the depths of winter there was life far more abundant than overturned brown earth in wait of another season. The few intelligible songs flowing from the pubs told of land and sea just as much, if not more than the losses of yesteryear. This was a country of life; yet death was not feared by most. Very few dwelled on the accumulated years so much as the quality of those they had. As I tripped, stumbled, and danced over these thoughts, my feet carried me up toward the cliffs edge. The ocean leapt over the rocks below with promises I could not yet comprehend, but I listened, sure enough, for a good hour before an inevitable downpour wrenched my head away and sent me striding back down into the city's grasp.

WHEN I RETURNED IT was not yet noon, yet one might have thought it evening by the sheer amount of people gathered together in the sitting room, and each keeping their hands at work. Catherine Keane, to my general astonishment, did not sit on the end of the couch near her husband's leather armchair, but had dragged her basket of yarn to the wooden stool in the corner and proceeded to knit. Her placement was nowhere near the practical position of the warm fireplace, nor the council of men. As I peeled my jacket from my shoulders, I noticed a third set of male eyes partially concealed beneath a dark shag of hair. He looked fairly young and might have struck me as tall if he were not so slumped forward against his knees. He was as far from Keane's age as he was mine, but no callus had seemed ever to so much as breathe on his hands. His pressed suit was new and arguably expensive, just a mild tan proved money enough to warrant a winter vacation to a place which most likely knew not the definition of snow. Thomas Keane pushed himself from his chair and laid a stiff hand on the young man's shoulder.

"Michael, this is Miss Joanna Lawrence. Miss Lawrence, my eldest son, Michael." I stood somewhat at bay, my mind staggered by such a proclamation. Of course, Keane had a brother—a married brother—in a Catholic country. I ought to have been more shocked if he did not have a nephew, niece, or any other lineage by his considerably older sibling. And yet, part of my mind still could not fathom the imagery of Keane playing the role of a doting uncle, nor had he ever struck me the man to sever his loyalties. The nephew, for indeed he was Keane's nephew, rose and grasped my outstretched hand with a natural show of disinterest, as if he could not decide if a woman is really a woman, even in trousers.

Keane muttered something incoherent from his position in a wood chair that sang painful ballads of a worse usage and Michael Keane immediately released my fingers in favor of fidgeting with the clip of his tie. Gold plated, I thought. I edged my way over to the other end of the couch, away from the nephew and where I was somewhat centered enough to make apt observations of this ill fitted feat of genetics. When nothing was said for a good few minutes; however, I began to regret not taking my chances with pneumonia, rather than most assuredly die of boredom. Unfortunately my fate was sealed when Mrs. Catherine Keane made it her duty as lady of the house to begin an utterly useless conversation with a guest on the verge of charging back out into the pouring rain.

"Brendan has informed me, Miss Lawrence, that your father was also from County Cork." I quickly agreed, then politely vomited the answers to several other uninteresting facts as well. My father's name was James O'Connor Lawrence. Yes, it was an interesting combination of Irish and French. No, I did not know where my French blood came from. (Though I suspected it was lounging about somewhere in my late maternal grandmother's lineage, rather than my father's.) Yes, my mother was an American. My maternal grandmother was, I thought, of German heritage. And finally; yes, I was a confirmed Catholic, but no, I was not married.

Keane managed to drag the conversation to some other topic as enthralling as the dismal weather before I was forced to disclose I had a second, partially removed cousin somewhere in the area of Dublin and an equally estranged relation who was brutally nicknamed "Pigeon" at some dark point of their youth. Gradually Keane's sister in law reclaimed the conversation but had the dignity enough to prattle on about some old woman who had—"God rest her soul"—died a month or so before. Never before had I appreciated the necessity of lunch preparation quite so much, as it delivered me from the hands of an over talkative woman into the dreary anti-socialism of three men. As the blanket of silence became comfortable, Thomas Keane pulled from his pocket a little leather purse and poured a string of beads into his calloused palm before fingering each bead individually.

A rosary is often a thing of mystery in and of itself. Some people regard it as an object of sentimental values, while others find it absurdly difficult to utter any sort of prayer without it. To most of the international population; however, it is a string of beads which blindly separates the Catholics from all society and condemns them to a prosecution fluctuated from a shortage of social invitations to a lack of anything above the neck. Thomas Keane's rosary was not out of the ordinary by any means. The once silver crucifix was now a light variation of brown, the black beads bore scrapes below dried clumps of wax, and few metal links had been crudely repaired. As the man's fingers shuffled along; however, you would have thought God himself had come down from Heaven just to place it in his work worn hands.

When his silent trek reached somewhere into the second decade, Michael abruptly rose and stalked from the room without so much as a grunt for apology. Keane did not glance up from the newspaper. His brother; however, paused between beads and addressed the rug spread in the middle of the floor.

"I don't know what to do with that boy." He growled deeply, and, had he not a rosary in his hand, I would have expected several more interesting words to have been lodged between those approved by English society.

"He is hardly a boy any more." Keane quipped. "And, as I recall, you were hardly blameless yourself at that age." The elder brother edged a little taller in his leather chair and instinctively continued edging his way along the beads between his fingers.

"I don't deny a fondness for drink now and again, but my crowd was always a good one, and I never once brought shame upon my family or country."

"Country?" I repeated as a sharp tingling sensation stabbed the back of my neck. The beads faltered for a moment.

"Brendan, are you still doing the mind thing to old soldiers?"

"Psychoanalysis."

"Aye, that. Do you think you could psycide—er—try it on Michael?" Keane abruptly lowered his newspaper; his blue eyes still piercing even behind a set of silver reading glasses. The elder brother shifted a little in his seat and allowed his fingers to slip back a bead. "It isn't I think he's gone mad, but he's in need of a few things straightened out in the muck of a brain shoved between his ears. Anthropology, for one thing. Who the devil pays good money to study society. A good bout in the pub can do it well enough, so. And for a meagre fraction of the price, might I say."

"Is that why you sent the letter?" Two pairs of eyes jerked toward me. The green ones stayed at my nose, and the blue ones gradually moved to look over my shoulder.

"Aye." The elder of the Keane brothers said at last with a swift glance to his junior who had again hidden himself behind his newspaper. Nothing more was said until Thomas Keane reached the end of his beads, poured them back into the little leather purse, and rose to excuse himself. As he reached the door, he turned round to face the two of us and I was startled to witness a nickname which had been created in a past to which I had proven myself incredibly naive.

"Bren?" The edge of Keane's newspaper relaxed and the sturdy features he had set throughout the whole of the conversation faltered for a brief instant. If I had blinked, I might have missed the brief moment before he gathered up the pieces and grunted as if to glue the shattered stone back together. His voice, however, was considerably more quiet and forgiving.

"Tell Michael to find me at four o'clock. If he comes... well, I shall see what I can do. *If* I can do anything."

WHEN THE HOUR ARRIVED I was forbidden to enter the sitting room; shunned from the work Keane and I had done to help dozens of soldiers and noblemen alike. And yet, I did not feel entirely dejected as I again wandered out into the streets. The rain had taken a brief moment to pause and collect itself, but, rather than again turning toward the openness of the countryside, I committed myself to the more inhabited portion. It was not terribly crowded so late in the afternoon. Much of the world had gathered up logic enough to barricade themselves within their homes; huddled behind blazing fireplaces and ovens. The joy of the new year was still somewhat apparent in the faces of those few I passed, but the merriment would soon be gone amidst a tone of memory. Hands clasping glasses of whiskey would again clutch tools of their trade and time would continue on as if it cared not for the sanctity of the moment.

And then I heard it: a hideous screeching erupting through the calm seas. It shattered all thought in the loudest decibels known to man. To think the culprit was no taller than my waist. An unfortunate woman worked desperately to quell the hysteric child, but the little boy seemed set on gaining the attention of all of Ireland and perhaps England as well. His little face was red and soaked with tears as his feet stamped into the ground. The woman tried all the usual bribes; sweets, coins, and, when these did not prevail, some childish threats. Perhaps the only bearable, even amusing thing to come of the situation was an old man near me, cursing furiously as he hunched over a sturdy walking stick. Apparently hearing loss was not one of his ailments. And then, without warning, the boy stopped his rampage and contented himself with sobbing heavily into his mother's skirts. His young hands groped at the fabric, but the woman dared not try to separate from him, else the world would once more be subjected to the child's screams. There was no doubt she had once been a beautiful woman, but age and motherhood had withered her away to a completion of sticky chalk with dark bags of stones hanging beneath her hazy eyes. What might have been a nice figure was now a bag of flesh and bones strung about without frame enough for recognition. She was a woman who seemed to care not for life, nor happiness, as she obviously believed them not to apply to her. Just as I swore myself never to become so helpless, she crumbled to the ground in a small, insignificant heap.

I HAVE HELD FEATHERS heavier and more substantial than the woman I was suddenly scraping from the pavement. She had not completely lost consciousness, but mumbled some excuse claiming she had forgotten to cook that day; yet, by looks alone, I might have suggested much longer. Five days perhaps? Certainly they had not seen a proper meal in over a fortnight. With one arm clutching her son, and the other grasping my shoulder, I suggested something to eat at a nearby pub, but her dirt ridden fingernails stabbed my flesh with the proposition. Fine.

On to plan two.

Our trek was slow and ground upon my famously short patience. The woman leaned heavily upon me, and the boy drug along behind her. Though it was not necessarily a difficult task, a thin layer of sweat began to cover my neck; becoming trapped between the wool and leather of my jacket and the frigid exterior of the world. It was a discomfort. A mild one, but a discomfort all the same. The tedium of the trek at last met its end as we reached the whitewashed door.

WHAM!

It took all my strength to prop the woman up as an unfortunately familiar figure wrenched the door from my hands, and my shoulder with it. My body surged forward; my right knee bashing into the door frame. Then Michael was gone, leaving a series of bruises in his wake. The little boy had been knocked off his feet and decided it was then perfectly acceptable to cry.

Loudly.

His mother had not the strength to console him; therefore, as I helped the woman into the house and explained the situation to Catherine, I allowed the wailing child to attach himself to the leg of the nearest unsuspecting individual.

Never had Keane looked so surprised.

CHAPTER THREE

"How was Michael?" It was really a ridiculous thing to ask; completely superfluous to the woman I half dragged to the house or the child who had to be peeled from Keane's trouser leg. But it was either suffer the effects of a tepid blunder or desperately hide a smile while staring at the wet blotches above my companion's knee. I was already in the midst of the latter; therefore, I found no reason not to do the first. It made no difference. Keane stepped around the question with all the grace of a man who had not gone without practice. He pulled a cigarette from its silver case; rolling it between his fingers before believing it sufficient enough to press between his lips.

"Lawrence, I never took you for the child who returned with unusual pets . . . but what am I to think?" He had always been condescending in the several years I had known him, but it was more often tedious than blatantly rude. I was not a child. Twenty-four is not a child. But God how I felt like one as he stared at me as though I was tiny and insignificant in his presence. He had always treated me as an equal, but now I was nothing. Nothing.

But no. There was something there. A glimmer of recognition. Some spark of familiarity to which I had first been captured by an incredible collection of complete intelligence. A lighthouse among the thrashing storm. For a brief instant, I questioned the amount of sheer energy required to power such mighty waves and allow the rain to pummel so heavily. Surely it could not last forever. He would have to become exhausted eventually.

But what if he didn't?

What if he remained this cold, dignified statue of a man? Could I live with that? Would I still be allowed to assist on his many theories and experiments?

Would I still be necessary?

I was thinking ludicrous imaginings. No. I wasn't thinking. I was sweaty, dirty, and tired: a miserable combination. I spun away from Keane and made a beeline for the staircase which would inevitably lead to a soft, warm, inviting bed. And yet, I paused.

"You are wrong." I corrected from the first step. "I am no longer a child, but when I was, I was the child who brought home lizards and frogs and snakes. I was the sort of adolescent who hid them in beds, nightstands, and equally unconventional places. That was why Charles died."

"Charles?"

"Charles the toad. Mother killed him when I was four." I practically ran up the short flight of stairs, flung open the guest room door, and stepped inside. There was some sanity, I thought, in its simpleness; therefore, I was at peace.

For about three seconds.

By the fourth second I was scavenging through my suitcase; grabbing handfuls of shirts, trousers, and socks, and hurling them at the wall.

When I first met Keane, I suspected his friendship was merely professional curiosity because he thought I was mad. It was, I suppose, possible. Perhaps I still was? In either instance, something snapped and I wanted only to leave the little, too-clean house and hide up in the greenery Ireland was so rightfully known for. If the nights got too cold or, heaven forbid, I became bored by such a feat . . . well, there was always England. And I did have a few manuscripts I needed to get to my editor.

Hell, if Keane wanted to make this a working vacation I could gather up my writing materials and scramble to the nearest pub. But the truth was my fingers ached from the constant pounding of typewriter keys. What knuckles were not sore were stained black with ink. My brain and imagination were completely involved in the confusion of this house. Between a conversational sister-in-law, a brother who made about as much sense as igloos in Arabia, and a nephew who had a few fire ants shoved down his shorts, I was at a complete loss as what to do with myself. In no circumstance did I fit into this picture. (It is difficult for an American to really "fit in" anywhere.) But here I was entirely out of place. Keane didn't even seem to recognize me. Or perhaps he chose not to.

I pushed my now empty suitcase to the wooden floor and took its place on the bed. God, what was I doing? I was twenty-four years old. An adult with money enough to go wherever I pleased, and, had the good Lord made me some twit with nothing between my ears, I might have had a chance with a number of men my age who could have blinded themselves to the fact I was not stereotypically attractive. I chuckled at the thought. No doubt I would come out looking better, and a great deal less bruised, had any man tried charming me. Charm, after all, is just a substitute for intelligence.

Cold, hard, wonderful intelligence . . .

I BELIEVE SUNDAYS WERE made for two distinct reasons; eternal salvation and complete boredom. While it is always a comfort to know there is something more than a black abyss when you die, I found myself struggling to remain still through the priest's homily in which hope was tossed about in the same raspy breath as sneezes, coughs, and, I suspected, a loose upper plate. If this alone was not enough, the woman behind me had no sense of pitch, but felt obliged to make up for it by singing so loudly she could not have remained on the correct note were she able. Thomas and his wife carried themselves through the entire mass with heads bowed low when in prayer and held high in song. When I risked a glance at Keane, I saw something entirely different. He followed through the Sunday ritual smoothly without missing so much as a single word. His hands were folded perfectly in his lap without even flinching toward his cigarette case. But he again seemed to be a thousand miles away in a land where I did not exist.

No one did.

At last we were set free apart from Thomas and Catherine's insistence we be introduced to all their friends, which were mercifully few. Keane bore the ritual with a graceful air that truly was himself; yet, rather than finding some excuse to leave while a handful of people discussed his clipped English articulation, he just stood there. Worse: he participated.

The collection of churchgoers gradually trickled outward toward the few splinters of sunlight where the churchyard spread outward to one side into a cemetery. Wedges of crumbling stone had been brutally stabbed into the ground with names and dates carved into their rigid surfaces. The letters were crude, but still somehow legible in the morning sun as I wandered from grave to grave. Every so often I would glare over where Keane stood against the church. His hands were still folded in front of him; not in his pockets, not holding his cigarette case. I was still unaccustomed to this older, boring stranger, and I despised him with every drop of blood coursing through my veins. Had he not neglected to acknowledge my presence, I might have been content hating him.

And then I saw it. Five letters etched deeply into a slab of grey. Five letters that immediately made me awestruck.

Keane.

Everyone has parents at some point in their life; however short an instance it may be. But there is never anything quite so spine chilling as facing a solid piece of evidence wedged into the frozen earth at your feet.

John Keane (1861-1901)

Fiona Keane (1883-1912)
Bridget Keane (1900-1905)

It was Thomas in the end who pulled me away from the cemetery and suggested we return to the house for lunch; yet, rather than climbing into the rickety, old automobile, he handed his younger brother the keys and placed a hand on my shoulder.

"I believe Miss Lawrence and I will walk back on such a glorious day such as this. No, Catherine me darlin, you go with Brendan and get the kettle boiling." As Keane drove off, the calloused hand slipped from my shoulder and linked to my arm, gently edging me forward into a long, slow walk. Thomas Keane was closer to my height than the towering form of his younger brother. In truth, they hardly looked alike at all. Where Keane's wavy hair was neatly combed and his face clean shaven, this man's hair was absurdly straight with a good deal of scruff covering his face. He was the devil's advocate of his brother, but perhaps the only other person I found moderately bearable at the moment.

St. Joseph's Church was tactfully stationed at the top of a hill with a single dirt road winding downward toward the city. When we reached bottom, he removed his heavy hand from my arm; yet, rather than turning toward his own home, he glanced at me with a roguish grin and pressed onward until I was thrust into a cloud of tobacco smoke which was rivaled only by stale beer and whiskey.

"God bless all here!" Thomas shouted into the joyous murk to which several equally hearty greetings emerged. We wove around conversations of horse racing, cattle, and, of course, the weather until we found an empty table splotched with dark amber stains. No sooner had I settled myself on a depressed chair than Thomas leaned forward on his elbows until his green eyes were level with mine.

"What do you fancy? A pint? Brandy?" I settled for half a pint and sat quietly while Thomas gave our orders to a ruddy-faced man, finishing with, "and I'll have me usual." As it happened, Thomas Keane's usual was a large dose of whiskey dumped into a glass and downed in a single gulp. As the empty cup was slammed back onto the table, a slow smile spread across the man's face.

"Good for the soul, that." He muttered across to me while another equally strong drink was set before him. "Hard to think you Americans refused to drink the stuff."

"Refused? Clearly you have never heard of Al Capone." The look on his face was familiar; utter shock immediately drowned in amusement. It was something I had seen a hundred times from his brother, but there was always some odd pleasure in it. Now I felt only as if I had tipped the scale far enough for it to crash from its chains. I had won.

"Brendan always said you were a sharp tongued lass." Thomas chuckled deeply. "Oh, he wrote a great deal about you and those adventures of yours. I'm pleased he brought you with him. I didn't think he would, tell the truth. I take it he didn't mention us though?" I swallowed a gulp of Guinness before slowly shaking my head. Rather than appearing angry, or even disappointed, the grey haired man raised the second whiskey to his lips and downed half of the brown liquid before setting it back on the table. "Can't say I'm much surprised. Everyone knew he would be the one to leave from the day he began strutting about practicing a posh English accent of his. Eire is in his blood, sure enough, but he wasn't the man who could settle down to farming or steel work or the like. I'm glad to see you've helped sand the edge off of him."

But that isn't Keane! I wanted to shout through the clouds of smoke. The scent of pipe tobacco was rancid, as it bore not the lightness of Keane's preferred cigarettes nor the assurance of his presence. I gripped my drink between both hands. All my knuckles grew frigid and pale. All that is, except for the smallest finger on my left hand, for which life and boxing had made nearly useless. My breath remained deep and strained, but controlled; always controlled.

"How long have you known my brother? Four . . . five years?"

"Almost seven." My answer was almost too fast; too prepared, as though I counted every moment. I took a breath and tried again. "I have known a Professor Keane for many years, but I cannot say I have been properly introduced to the man who brought me here." The man who won't smoke. The man who is content to read the same newspaper for over half an hour. The man who has a brother.

And then there was this other man with the unshaven face who leaned forward slightly across the table—the abyss—separating us. It was I who ran to the bridge.

"Who was Bridget?" Thomas downed his whiskey, ordered another, and finished it with the same speedy efficiency. His green eyes looked everywhere, at anyone who did not bear the Lawrence name. It was not until I had bought another round of strong alcohol his answer came, scarcely above a whisper.

"She was our sister. Broke through the ice on a pond when she was five." He leaned back, closed his eyes, and muttered something under his breath. It took me a moment to realize it was in Irish. "Damn fool of a brother didn't go to the funeral!"

This near shouted phrase solidified two things securely in my mind. The first was that Keane had a more tightly-knit family than I ever suspected. And second, his brother was very drunk indeed.

I HAD ALWAYS KNOWN Keane to be a man of many passions and interests. He was musical in the sense he understood it and therefore was appreciative. I was always convinced Shakespeare had written just that men such as he may read and find beauty in it. And yet, I found Keane in the guest room with another damn newspaper spread across his lap and a cold cup of tea resting on the nightstand. Not a breath stirred. I sat down on the edge of my own bed and snatched up a book I had abandoned that morning. It was the perfect size and weight to fling across the room and knock the final tea dregs onto the floor. This I did not do, but nor did I press it far from my mind.

"I believe I can forgive you for not telling me of your brother. I might also understand why you never mentioned that rogue son of his. However, to not tell me of Bridget—" The name was enough. Keane's head jerked upward and the printed papers spilled to the floor. His fingers flew to his pockets in a deft search; smacking his tweed clothing in desperation. "Is this what you want?" I held the weapon of self destruction open in my palm.

Keane glared at the object, as though it had betrayed him by allowing its cold, smooth metal to sit regally on my hand. When it did not leap to him, he snatched it to himself and began smoking the cigarettes feverishly; one after another. Eventually he flung open the single window and settled himself on the ledge. Long, deep puffs of smoke billowed from his lips and wandered into the Irish landscape. With each finished butt that fell below, my friend returned. I shifted against the wall.

"I am sorry she died."

"She didn't die."

"But your brother—"

"My brother is a fool!" He roared. For a long moment there was only silence dotted with the quiet hiss of matches. When yet another cigarette was going, his voice returned, this time taunt with control. "You have heard of schizophrenia?" I nodded. "She had it. The kindest soul you would have ever met and God gave it to her. But she was a fighter. There was a time—oh, she must have been no more than four at the time— when she wrestled the neighbor's dog when it growled at her." A faint smile flickered across his lips. "You would have liked Bridget."

"I'm sure."

"When I returned from Dublin, they told me she had wandered out into the snow, broke through some ice, and drowned. It wasn't until nearly four years later I learned the truth. They had locked her up in an asylum. A kind, innocent little girl behind bars like the murderers; alone in the dark because she could see and hear a world all to herself." Keane drew a long drag from his cigarette before releasing it in a thin, restrained line. "I bought her a doll for her fifth birthday. A little thing with buttons for eyes and red hair made from strands of yarn. She refused to go anywhere without it. They said she was still clinging to it when they put her into the cart and—"

He broke off, unable to continue further into his thoughts. I waited through the silence. When he was again able to continue, his voice was deceptively reasonable. Lethal.

"I went to visit her once. She looked so small in that room; so pale and thin one might have thought her a ghost. It was like those final moments before a body succumbs to a cancerous tumor. They wouldn't allow me to enter the room. Claimed she was too dangerous and mad to see anyone. Yet, they had injected her with so many opiates and its evil spawn she could not have bruised a bug, let alone recognize me . . ." Keane took a sharp huff of air. " As far as I know, or am permitted know, she is still living in a Hell that has killed the strongest of men." It was here Keane stopped, not for lack of things to say or memories too horrid to describe, but something more practical.

He was out of cigarettes.

The majority of his rage had fallen away, leaving him looking tired and ill. For the first time within the visit, I questioned whether he had been sleeping, as dark circles surrounded his eyes. He slipped his cigarette case into its assigned pocket before trampling on the newspapers to grab his coat and hat. An unfortunate part of me was prepared for him to stalk out the door and once more fall into play as the strange brother. The carefully measured act that forbade cigarettes and shunned that ever constant twinkle from his turquoise-grey eyes. I had not expected that gentle hand on my elbow, my leather jacket shoved into my arms, or the door opening and shutting behind us.

CHAPTER FOUR

I awoke some time during the night to the screams and wails of an overactive mind. There is nothing quite so troublesome as an imagination at work. For a writer such as me, it is pure Hell. After a time, I pulled the bedclothes back over my ears and compelled myself to drift lazily away into the silence of sleep. When at last the morning showed its fiery head, I was shocked by one of the most horrendous things known to humankind. I was half frozen.

The floorboards bit into my bare feet and the air nipped at my skin. Every inch of me screamed for the blessings of a hot bath; however, the faucets ran cold. An hour or so later, when I staggered stiffly down the stairs, I found the fireplaces baring only the faintest gleam of glowing embers. The only true warmth wafted from the kitchen in the scent of baked bread. Beyond that, a steady thump was the only proof of life at all. I cut away a slice of the hot bread and had just begun to smother it with butter when the thumping abruptly stopped and the door was flung open. The man who staggered in was so unlike himself in every way it was impossible not to laugh.

"Kindly stop that snickering, Lawrence, before that butter drips all over your shirt." Keane collapsed into the nearest kitchen chair without removing his heavy coat, hat, or the mud stained boots a few sizes too large.

"What on earth were you doing galavanting around out in the cold?"

"Catherine needed more firewood cut." He heaved, rubbing at his frozen face before coughing heavily into his fist. "My word. I haven't had this much exercise in weeks." I handed him a cup of tea.

"Not up for a walk through the country then?"

"I am momentarily tired, Lawrence, not a blasted invalid. Beastly temperature, though."

Beastly was hardly the word for it. Every inch of land had suddenly froze with the passing of a single night. The rich smell of earth had dissipated into that of winter's icy hand. Each step furthering ourselves from the city carried us deeper into the crisp country outlook, very much like that I had explored on my first morning. Rather than leading up toward the rigid whitewashed cliffs and roaring ocean; however, Keane took my arm and turned downward toward a great expanse of towering trees. Their barren bows nodded their heads as we passed beneath them. To them we had gained nobility above most, for we knew them by name and respected them forthwith. Where my feet trampled cautiously along the uneven bits, Keane's continued steadily and swiftly. He had forgone his brother's oversized boots for his own shoes, while Catherine had insisted with every feminine emotion that I borrow her worn leather footwear that was not only too small at the toes but was to be a guaranteed breeding ground for blisters. Suddenly the great throng of noble trees grew outward around a great, silver pond. The seemingly endless surface only faltered around a large trunk grasping at the clouds. No two grown men could wrap their arms about the giant, for indeed it was unconquerable. Even so, had it not been so devilishly cold, I might have swam across and risked both neck and limb to clamber into the safety of it's branches.

Keane stepped forward toward the water's twinkling edge, removed his hat, and opened his arms to greet the somber surrounding:

"*In mist or cloud, on mast or shroud,*
It perched for vespers nine;
Whiled all the night, through fog-soaked white,

Glimmered the white moon-shine."

His voice, which was naturally rich and full, darted along the bark of trees until it became but a deep whisper among them. When he stopped speaking, he was applauded by a sharp breeze that whipped through his well combed hair.

I was struck. "You've been to the top of that tree? Haven't you?" Keane turned toward me; his eyes glimmering like the water behind him as he grinned down at me.

"Indeed, though it was a might more difficult coming down." He reached his long fingers up toward his right temple and held a bit of his thick, greying hair away to disclose the near invisible remnants of a scar running jaggedly for a few inches before again darting beneath his hairline. For the briefest instant, I saw a young boy standing at my feet; thin and gaunt with one of the most treasured awards of childhood cut in red on a familiar face. At my startled expression, Keane's humor faded and the grey hat once more returned to his head.

"Out with it, Lawrence, before you burst with that curious energy of yours."

"I was just thinking what you must have been like when you were—when you were younger?" His eyes jerked to mine, which happened to be searching for something—anything—other than his.

"You would have found me conceited and priggish. Just ask my brother."

"And that's another thing. For the past seven years I was convinced you had no remaining family; yet, now you admit to, not only a brother and sister, but a nephew as well."

"And a twice removed cousin in New Jersey."

"Keane, I'm serious!" My companion smiled gently and leaned casually against an ancient tree as he reached for his cigarette case. Amongst his plethora of talents, ignoring my fury was often lounging near the top of the list. His fingers freed one single cigarette before lazily diving into his pocket for some means to light it, though he appeared just as eager to allow a bolt of lightning to do the job as he would some society approved means. At last the end glowed orange.

"What is it you wish to know?"

"Do you have any other siblings?"

"No."

That was sufficient enough for Keane to relish his cigarette in silence before beginning another. Rather than allowing this one to dangle from his lips; however, he held it in his hand to speak.

"I am fond of my family. But people grow, Lawrence. They change. And one must accept it and move on. All relationships, family or otherwise, are much the same. You can't capture perfection between people just as it is impossible to stop time. Some bonds last forever, while others . . ." The rest of his words dispersed in a cloud of white smoke before being crushed violently beneath his heel. I was so preoccupied in this sudden change in emotion, I was unaware that Keane had tucked my arm in his and began leading back toward the foot worn path.

We had not gone far when my foot twisted over a root and, had it not been for my companions quick balance and arm linked to mine, I would have been sprawled face down on the frozen earth. As it was, his elbow jabbed into my ribs and left me gasping for breath.

"I'm alright. It's these damn boots. They're too—" And then I saw it.

Strange, how long it took my mind to comprehend the picture before me. But it was all wrong. So much out of place with some pieces missing entirely. Even beneath the blood caked clothes I understood this was to be one of the most harrowing sights of my mere twenty-four years. There were no feet or ankles attached to the legs that stuck from the torso at a sickeningly unnatural angle. The wrists had not been tied, but severed completely of hands and fingers. A large tear down the front of the shirt opened around exposed organs seeping from enormous slits through flesh. Fortunately, the face had been left better intact, apart from a large gash at the neck. There was a small mouth, a nose, and two eyes. But oh, those eyes; two balls of glass fogged over by death's touch.

It was the screaming boy.

PART TWO

Do not resent growing old.
Many are denied the privilege.
-Irish Proverb

CHAPTER FIVE

In the valuable time it took to assess these grievous sins against the laws of anatomy, Keane had torn off his overcoat and draped it respectfully over the child's body. Somewhere between the rushing of blood through my ears and a threatening grey in my vision, the Garda leapt from behind the trees and began swarming around the ravaged remains like vultures. A gangly youth much too scrawny for his uniform, bounded from tree to tree with a notebook that still had all its pages.

I emitted a sharp gasp between my teeth as my companion's coat was stripped from the wreckage of humanity. The inner lining had dried slightly to the boy's bloody shirt; causing the corpse to jerk upward suddenly before again slamming into the ground like a mound of cold rubber. Had the body been a bit fresher, I could imagine the thick, red substance spewing from the severed limbs into the dark ground. Frozen and hard like the bare bone visible where his hands and feet ought to have—

Suddenly there was a hand on my arm pushing me backward toward a bare tree stump. The grasp, though not entirely painful, was that of iron and it took me a good, long moment before I was able to break away.

"I am not about to faint, Keane." I hissed in a voice that reeked of steady confidence, something my boiled legs certainly did not feel as they dragged themselves across the hard earth.

"I did not think you would," my companion whispered calmly as his strong, thin hand again appeared between my shoulder blades. "I merely thought you may wish to sit down." And sit I bloody well did. Hard.

As I closed my eyes and leaned my head back against the bark of yet another tree, I was aware of a second weight settling beside me. The tweed of his jacket brushed against my shoulder as his fingers delved in and out of his pockets. Eventually, the recognizable scent of tobacco flitted about my head until I could taste the bitter cloud. It was a good smell. Entirely masculine. Like the dignity of a gentleman and sweat of a cad.

I snatched Keane's silver case and brought one of the paper cylinders to my lips. My head bowed to a flickering match before again sitting back against the rough wall of bark. As breathing became natural again, the solidness of the smoke rushing in and out of my mouth slowly relaxed the rest of my muscles. The bitter taste was nothing in comparison to its strength and I finished the cigarette more aware of my surroundings than before, but though the shock had worn away, the sick feeling in my stomach continued to lurch as the corpse was loaded into the back of a market wagon that would take it up the path to the main road. The young, spindly man in uniform pelted us with questions until he was dragged away by his superiors. Would we care for a ride back to town? No, we would walk. Even so, Keane had the courtesy to wait until all other curious persons disappeared before shifting about on the stump; his icy blue eyes searching for something more substantial than the few wisps of smoke still malingering in the air.

"Lawrence, I could use a drink."

THE PUB WAS INCREDIBLY busy as the lunch hour was well upon us. Smells of sweat and other decidedly masculine odors attacked my nasal passages with more vitality than any smelling salts. What the cigarette began the roar of boisterous laughter finished in one great attempt at reinstalling some normality to my life. But that was all it was, or could have been. An attempt. My appetite had long since vanished with the poor boy's feet and hands, but that did not stop the rest of society from enjoying thick, greasy foods accompanied by an inevitably large amount of alcohol.

As soon as a round of whiskey lay before us, Keane made certain that every man to pass our table enjoyed the same. If that made their tongues a little looser and information a bit freer, so be it. I could have gathered enough material for a dozen novels after an hour or so; ghosts, fairies, ill grandmothers, suspicious deaths, and even a lost dog story from a man who had particular trouble holding his liquor. It was during this story I became increasingly interested in the group at the other end of the pub.

They were not drunk, necessarily, merely overzealous at every word uttered among them. In the middle of the self proclaimed society sat a scruffy old man with a threadbare coat hung in semi-woven patches about his shoulders. He had at least four beers under his belt, not taking into account the half filled glass held in his hand. To say it was held might have been an understatement. With every motion of his arm the pale liquid sloshed outward; often leaping from the frothy rim onto the soiled floorboards. At one moment of his youth, he might have possibly been considered strong. Not handsome by any means, but perhaps muscular. Age and time now made it impossible to tell, for what might have been a cunning figure had ballooned into obesity.

Keane finally managed to convince the other man, who had become a blubbering mass over the loss of his dog, to go tell the story to some equally intoxicated chap slumped over an empty glass. (Though, from the way his arms clung to his stomach, I wagered that the glass would again be filled very soon, this time with a thick, pungent substance.) I tore my eyes away and back to where Keane sat. That is, where he had sat. I found myself faced with an empty chair and a bitter frustration that gradually softened to amusement when I again caught a glimpse of his slender frame speaking rather loudly to the enormous gentleman with the beard. (A statement, I soon realized, accounted for the vast majority of the pub's inhabitants.) The rich clip of Keane's speech was matched evenly with the other's obtuse slurs. Word for word, drink for drink, it continued on through an hour's wake. As my companion succeeded to remain on his feet and keep the drunken fog from his eyes, the man who was three—perhaps four times his size began to slip further into complete inebriation. I casually edged my way around the pub until I was standing near Keane's shoulder. Between the intelligible ribbons of words and unintended spoonerisms, I waited for the bearded man's attention to slip away for an instant; just enough time to swipe an empty glass from a nearby table to replace the half filled one drooping from Keane's thin hand. His nimble fingers migrated upward toward the rim where a bright red smudge of lipstick was all too apparent. Not that his action mattered much, of course. The other man was too far gone to notice me standing there, let alone a discrepancy the size of a thumbnail.

My companion leaned back against the wall with his long legs incredibly steady for a man who had consumed such devastating amounts of alcohol. His eyes were still clear, though they wandered around a bit through the man's intelligible ramblings. As actors went, I had long since accepted Keane as one of the finest in all the world, but, when suddenly caught the slightest slip of a vowel when it was again his turn to speak, I remembered there was only so much liquor one could spill on the floor.

"Now, about the information you promised me about that young boy." Keane managed, his 't's a bit less articulate than usual. The bearded man waved a hand and fresh glasses quickly appeared before them; white foam dripping over the sides. And so the games began.

I HAD SEEN KEANE PLAY many amusing roles in our seven years. I had foolishly thought myself to have seen every possible performance; the soldier, sailor, priest, beggar, crippled old man, government agent, and about three or four high ranking officials, but not at the same time, nor in that particular order. Though I would always bear a deep fondness for all of these mentioned, none would prove quite so memorable as the groaning figure sitting on the edge of the bed with his skull mashed between his hands.

"Lawrence!" He hissed through the gaps of his fingers. "If you insist to be so helpful as to bring me some tea, put it down carefully and quietly."

"I *am* sorry. Would it help more if I just poured the steaming contents in your lap. You'd be on your feet in no time at all." To prove my point, I made no effort to soften the thump of my steps on the floorboards as I marched back to my bed and tested the springs a bit when I sat down. What a pleasure it was to see Keane visibly flinch with each little screech until two bloodshot eyes glared up at me.

"Have I ever complimented your sense of humor?" I smiled wickedly.

"No, Keane, I don't believe you have."

"Good." His head immediately dropped back into his hands; an action that appeared to do little more than cause a string of curses to seep from his lips. "God, this is bad."

"Are you certain you don't want me to pour that tea on you? No? How about some nice half-frozen water then. Seems like all we can get with this blasted temperature—"

"Lawrence!" Keane growled deeply before his head dutifully reminded him of the activities of the day prior. Not that it took much for me to notice from my perch across the room. His hair had long since freed itself from pomade and the slightest shadow of facial hair threatened his well defined jaw. The grey tweed jacket had been slung over the bedpost with one of the sleeves touching the floor right beside his necktie. I could only see one shoe lying on its side under the nightstand. His braces had been freed from his shoulders and hung on either side of his waist, while his severely wrinkled shirt had come untucked completely. Perhaps his only consolation was in the strength of his stomach.

"Well, at least you got the information you wanted." I offered gently. Keane took the bait.

"Did I?"

"Why, don't you remember?" A slow smile spread across my face. "Though I think that man was too sloshed for it to be viable. Tell me again, Keane, as an Irishman, what are the chances of a group of fairies leading the boy away into the forest." The only answer was another series of odd noises as he painfully reached over to his discarded jacket and carefully worked to free his silver case. When he found that empty (announcing the fact with a fresh selection of Irish curses best left to the more rowdy parts of town) I rose and grabbed a spare package of cigarettes from his luggage. Oh the temptation to fling the paper box across the room, but, being the kindhearted person I was, I contented myself with traveling the distance with a few heavy strides before slamming it down on the nightstand; forcing the priorly stationed teacup to rattle violently in his ears.

"Damn it all, woman!"

"Ah ha! So you remember I am a woman. Allow me to remind you then of the condescending stares and suggestive looks as I dragged you out of the pub and down the street. In broad daylight no less."

"I didn't think you paid head of society's idiotic mutterings, or the fact much of the human population has followed the tradition of having a pair of eyes. Transcendentalism and all that."

"I don't, nor do I take residence in the arguably useless well of romanticism." The man hunched over in front of me worked up enough bravery to pry his splitting head from his hands.

"Is there something I ought to know?" I sighed and edged my way quietly toward the door.

"Never mind, Keane." Never mind the odd looks from half the men in County Cork, or the fact I had best be on my guard for any young men too forward for their own good. God, what nuisances men could be. I stopped with my hand on the frosty door knob. Damn temperature. "Now, who would you like to shave you this morning; me, your brother, Catherine . . . or would you rather run the risk of slitting your own throat?"

I didn't wait for the answer. I slammed the door behind me. Hard. I could almost hear the rude phrases smash to the floor, along with almost every bit of sanity the man had left on that particular morning.

IT WAS NOT UNTIL THE clock in the kitchen timidly edged past eleven that Keane made his appearance. His hair had been carefully combed to its usual style and, by some miracle, he had shaven without any angry wounds running along his face. A fresh tweed suit, only slightly darker than its successor, had been chosen out of a handful of others, and, considering the shade of his trousers was the same musty grey I had seen for the past several hours, my brain needed hardly flinch to know why.

"He's alive! Send the undertaker away!" Thomas rumbled as his younger brother cautiously entered the room. Clearly I wasn't the only one willing to have some fun with the unusual situation. (Just so long as the tables didn't overturn any time in the near future.) Catherine shuffled around the tea kettle and handed a fresh cup to Keane, who was excruciatingly careful to keep the steaming liquid well out of my reach as he picked his way through a plate of toast and eggs. Little was said, though I was unsure if it was from lack of words or the blatant fact any other unwelcome noise would drive my companion to something drastic, and no doubt lethal to Catherine's simple, white dishes. Thomas was the first to leave under the logical excuse of work. His wife's sudden need for her knitting was unimaginative, but she still escaped unscathed by any tongue. I did not expect to be so fortunate. Nor was I so cowardly as to retreat.

"I do hope your plans today do not involve searching for little blips of light flitting about the forests." I jested lightly; spearing a bit of egg on my fork and allowing it to mop up a puddle of yoke that had edged dangerously close to the singed pieces of bread.

"You do me a great disservice with those childish comments of yours, Lawrence. I would not dare do such a thing myself. No, I will learn all I can about the boy, while *you* will go back to the forest and—"

"You can't be serious!" I exclaimed; allowing the silver utensil in my hand to clatter noisily against the plate. And though it had not been my intention, my anger was slightly appeased by my companions violent reaction to the disturbance. His thin fingers slipped upward and began to massage his greying temples.

"Do I not look serious?"

"But really, Keane! Fairies—"

"Did I say that was the purpose of the errand? Really, Lawrence, do try to control that imagination of yours. Or at least save it for those books you insist on writing." I fingered the four pronged utensils in my hand, wondering what Irish law had to say about attacking one's companion with a fork. Nothing too painful, of course; just enough to force all those ridiculous creatures of folklore from his otherwise incredible brain. He might as well send me out in the damn cold with a paper bag and tell me to catch a leprechaun.

I forced a smile and leaned forward against the wooden table until my elbows complained of the rough surface.

"And, what, pray tell, does one look for when hunting for the little creatures? Trails of pixie dust?"

CHAPTER SIX

The name Brendan Keane could open any door in Devon, make the world of psychoanalysis bend at his hand, and cause even the most senior of constables to clamber beneath a blanket of self-conscious twitching. To Sergeant Walsh; however, it meant another middle-aged meddler with little more experience in official Homeside than the Irish terrier dozing peacefully beneath a much abused desk. It was not until the title of 'Professor' less than tactfully entered the single ended conversation that the man recognized his existence. This meant the better portion of yet another hour was wasted in the explanation of psychology and that it was indeed not among the useless professions of the world.

The sergeant, still pending judgement on the latter, shuffled his words around a stack of month old newspapers.

"Like I've been say'n, you'd be wasting your time on that wee chiseler."

"Would I indeed?" Keane glared down at the man at least two decades his junior, who had the grace enough to at least look mildly discomforted by the two dark storms thundering above him.

"Sure ya would, God rest his soul. That loony mother of his chopped him to bits b'for jumping off a cliff. Pulled her body from the water this morn'n."

"I assume the coroner would agree with your deductions?"

"Er—"

"And you have sufficient evidence to bring the matter to court without the slightest shadow of a doubt?"

"N—"

"That's what I thought, so if you would be so kind as to show me both corpses and the necessary files—"

"You're mad!" The uniformed man exclaimed; sending the small dog at his feet bolting to the opposite side of the room. "I can't just be show'n evidence to a civilian. If I did, every drunk and busybody would be prowlin' at me door. Then where would I be but play'n host to a collection of dirt." The sergeant's irritatingly shrill voice had heightened into a near shout the further he argued his case. However, unlike the cowardly terrier, Keane leaned forward over the desk until his angular face was mere inches from the officer's.

"A young boy—a child—is dead. And if by some strange twist of fate you have uttered something of a truth, his mother is as well. Would you wish for these misfortunes to forever simmer on that flimsy piece of flab you call a conscience? Do you wish to have those ill-gotten insignias torn from your uniform? No?" The sergeant squirmed beneath the older man's steely gaze. Though his moral value may have left something to be desired, his nervous fingers could not resist fingering the extra patches decorating his shoulders. At last there came a strained sigh that sounded more at home coming from a wounded feline than the lips of a fully grown man.

"What files did ya be want'n?"

IT WAS LESS THAN A quarter of an hour later that Keane excited the Garda station with a thick envelope clutched beneath his arm and directions to the coroner's surgery fresh in his brain. Even through the murk of the sergeant's inability to communicate anything of importance to his fellow men, it was not long before he reached a cream colored building with crumbling steps only marginally better in shape than the woman who opened the door. Surely there are gargoyles stationed upon the great Notre-Dame Cathedral that are far more appealing to the eye. She lurched to one side and gruffly stationed Keane in an absurdly small sitting room made from pieces of furniture that had no logical resemblance to its neighbors. There were a variety of bookshelves, but they contained nothing more entertaining than an obituary column. When at last the coroner appeared, he appeared much in the same state. It was of little surprise then when his rough voice betrayed his foreign homestead. Mainly, he was British.

The muscles of a corpse, once passing through rigor mortis, slacken again; pinning two sheet covered parcels to their separate slabs. Keane went first to the smaller of the two. The white cloth stretched and folded to cover the mutilated mound of flesh that, even in the frozen temperatures, had slowly begun to rot beneath the woven grave. With deliberate care, Keane folded the sheet back only so far as the boy's collar bone; exposing those gentle features of youth drained of all color and maimed by fear. The gouging wound lay open as a second, larger mouth saying all he no longer could.

Murder.

Keane meticulously began examining what remained of the youth; tugging the sheet further down as he worked. But he had seen it all the day before: slices through the torso that exposed punctured internal organs; bones, not only broken, but smashed completely, the ends of wrists and ankles crudely severed by a dull instrument. The sheet was quickly replaced over the rubberized flesh and Keane stepped to the second slab.

There is a difference between men and women, far larger and more important than the basic oppositions of anatomy. A woman risks many things in her life to which the slightest slip of footing proves fatal.

Were she to choose the path of strength formerly classified too masculine or eccentric to be accepted into the drab walls of society, she often aged to spinsterhood, or worse, chained to the bane of humanity as a wife to the hopeless husband.

Were she to travel the path of perfection; to sway upon the stones set by everyone except herself, she becomes someone else entirely and thereby never knows the joys of life or the fulfilling richness of living, rather than staring into the abyss of existence.

Then there is the lowest of low, as society so often dictates. Upper classes look down upon them; forgetting they are not below them, but a part of them they wish never to disclose. The woman who sleeps in another man's bed to escape poverty is more often forgiven than the woman who does so out of insecurity. In either case, the results are just as devastating as the act. What dignity remains in a woman is lost and respect shatters upon middle class floorboards.

Keane pulled the sheet to the floor in one swift motion and it was by her face alone he knew all too well she was the third option. The last path of life. The paint on her face had washed away in some places, while clinging still at the eyes and mouth. The deep reds served as the only colors that had not been leached from her fragile features. Great knots of dark hair clung to her head in wet tangles and her neck was spotted with dark bruises. In size, she was little more than a skeleton; flesh bloated from hours in water.

"And you say she committed suicide?"

"Aye. Jumped off the cliff herself."

"Then what is this?" Keane gingerly lifted a gnarl of wiry, sand coated hair; revealing a deep wound bashed into the skull just above the right temple. It was clean; however, and rounded evenly inward at the sides.

"She hit a cluster of rocks before striking the water. Really, I should say that was rather obvious."

"Obvious or not, I have yet to see a rock so perfectly circular and elongated." The doctor stiffened considerably; the crown of his balding head scarcely reaching the top of Keane's ear.

"There is no reason to think it murder. A woman of her—Er—profession would not be worth dangling from a rope." Keane gradually covered the woman's scrawny form with the white sheet; pausing briefly before allowing the cloth to fall over her partially painted face.

"And yet there was Jack the Ripper."

CHAPTER SEVEN

When I had first met Keane, I believed him to be the most condescending, prideful, and irritating man ever to walk the earth. Therefore, I liked him. Not necessarily for the items formerly mentioned, but because he was completely his own man without his hands bound to the world. He was a man of the mind; quiet in thought but sharp of wit. His humor too was always a part of him and often appeared at the most unusual of times. But, for all his gentleness and intelligence, there was no doubt in my mind that he would never be assaulted sitting down. It was for all these things I liked him.

And now I hated him.

I hated him through the morning frost so prominent on the darkened ground. I hated him in the forestry that hunched over bow-like canes. Most of all, I hated him for sending me out into the frozen wilderness to examine the deathbed of a child I had met only days before. The boy was alive then. Alive as he screamed on the street. Alive as he trudged alone beside his mother. Alive as he sobbed into Keane's trouser leg.

Many of those who live long lives welcome death with open arms and hearts yearning for eternal rest, while the young fear icy hands groping blindly for their throat. This child knew nothing of these things, for youth so fresh knows only of life as it is in a single instant. Tomorrow and yesterday are immaterial to them. There is only today. This moment.

Now.

My momentum through the shrubbery at last faltered as the grey pond rippled through my vision. In the space of two steps I had stopped completely. There, not four feet from my own, stretched a deep glaze of rusted earth. A haze of darkened red had encrusted in frost and cried out with the sharp glint of a knife. The sun, though concealing all warmth from this horrible world, caught every bit of nauseating clarity; lumps of death's color cracked with age and created the foggy silhouette of a life cut short by steel's fatal claws. For the briefest instant I saw the deep and fatal wounds; a crude instrument severing the hands and feet from an innocent. I heard the hollow sound of metal lacerating human flesh. The wetness of life's thick liquid splattered easily upon the hands and face of the attacker and spilled downward into little streams. The brown dirt greedily lapped at the blood until it grew red with it. Where the sticky globs did not dry, it froze into gnarled fingers gripping toward the earth's surface.

A cold, stale vomit coated my throat and edged forward toward my tongue. I turned my back on the scene of such misery and did not return to myself until I had briskly walked halfway around the pond. It was an extraordinarily large body of water; small enough to easily see the other side yet there was no doubt to its immense depth. Even with the tree growing out of the middle, it was a masterpiece; still, calm, and completely unlike the waves thrashing beneath stoney cliffs. How like Keane it was and, for the briefest instant, I could see the spindly boy he once had been dangling from the tree's highest branches. Two thin legs wrapped clung to the trunk as he grinned in victory. A sailor up the mizzen mast would look much the same. Keane had said returning to the ground had been harder. It always is. But there is some pride in it as well, for no boy becomes a man without a few scars.

CHAPTER EIGHT

Halfway to the house, the temperature plummeted further still; freezing my various limbs far more thoroughly than comfort could ever condone. By the time I staggered through the door, my legs no longer wished to bend to my will and the few fingers that had not gone numb were ones rarely used by humankind. This was soon remedied by a long bath, somewhat warmed by a few pots of water boiled over the stove. I scrubbed my skin vigorously from head to foot, submersed myself, then repeated the ordeal. Feeling sufficiently cleansed, I then lay back in utter paradise; confident that the world still retained some fleeting glimpse of sanity. The rest of the house seemed to be a different matter entirely.

I was aware of a door opening and closing with a force that caused the aching wood to groan, shouts that would set a deaf man reeling, and, as time passed, the lightest traces of tobacco mingling sociably with tea leaves.

Though it was inevitable, I was nonetheless saddened when the bath turned frigid. Quickly I clambered out of the water and proceeded to dry the moisture from my limbs lest it turn to ice. Then, separating my warmer clothing from those assuring pneumonia, I settled on a thick wool sweater and my heaviest trousers. No doubt I looked like some unfortunate fisherman, but I would always be a live fisherman rather than the dead fish wrapped in ice.

Clean, warm, and feeling better than I had in days, I nodded to the fisherman in the looking glass and trudged toward the stairs.

KEANE HAD SETTLED HIMSELF on the sitting room floor surrounded by loose papers and photographs of varying freshness. An overflowing ashtray lay at his feet and, by the large assortment of dishes, it was safe to assume the consumption of several cups of tea and the better portion of a bottle of brandy. A new overcoat had been casually slung over a wicker chair, along with several packs of cheap cigarettes. Fortunately the sofa was not in use apart from a single photograph taken of the murder scene I had spent the past several hours scouring. I pinched the edge between the tips of my fingers before promptly dropping it into Keane's lap.

"There is nothing quite like a death to make a holiday interesting."

"Two. The mother was found this morning."

"Oh." Keane slipped the silver reading glasses onto his nose and shuffled through various documents before finding a small collection of photographs still held together by a single paperclip. He plucked the first from the metal bondage and tossed it to me.

"Tell me, Lawrence, what do you see?" It was a simple question. Absurdly simply; yet, through the dark smudges and fading light it took a moment to find an answer.

"Obvious water damage, a strong bash to the side of her head, and something smeared on her face."

"Paint. Cosmetics. There was sand in her hair as well." The next picture flew to me. This time the ink portrayed upwards from the woman's prominent collar bone. Unfortunately, either the photographer was new to the profession, or he had a weak stomach.

"Keane, those smudges on her neck. If they are bruises, then she was—"

"Murdered. Yes. Most likely she was held underwater close to shore."

"Which would explain the sand." I agreed, laying the photographs beside me. My companion pushed himself up from the cold floor and threw his frame into the leather armchair; the wooden feet rocking violently with the impact. "I take it the guards have some distasteful theory?"

"Distasteful?" Keane growled. "Distasteful is hardly the word for it. The imbeciles claim a mother would mutilate her child for the sheer joy of it. A madness, they say. Queer in the head, they say. Those light brained idiots would say anything for their convenience."

"Surely there must be some—"

"What? Truth? They don't know the meaning of the word. Any scratch of truth lulling about their empty heads died at the sight of paint upon the woman's face. Do you know, Lawrence, there wasn't a pub hell hole in a ten mile radius who had seen her for the past five years. She had pulled herself from that life through a determination foreign to the rest of society. But she had succeeded . . . only to be murdered and convicted by a little womanly paint."

"But think of those five good years." I argued gently. "Surely that is of some comfort to her soul." A heavy sigh shook my optimism until the wall's edges began to crumble downward into dust. And yet, Keane caught the remains and molded them between his wisened hands.

"There is some truth in what you say, but what is obvious to you and I is often ignored by the rest of the world."

I counted the cigarette butts condemned to the fireplace as Keane erratically puffed and blew all life from the little wraps of paper. One. Two. Three. Four. But it was on the fifth one his fingers no longer flicked the butt to the flames. Rather, he dropped it; seemingly unaware of the dangers of allowing one's hand so close to fire's mighty tongues. It was superfluous now. To one who sees such death, it is an everlasting battle not to tumble into the abyss of thick murk. I had no fear for Keane, nor myself. Our paths had been forged in the fires of suffering, and thereby strong enough to carry us to long life and, God willing, a natural death far from man's spindly hands. It was a theory, of course, but I believed it was a good one. A strong one. A true one. But as each cigarette was drained and discarded, the moments did too pass into hours of heavy silence pressing about my ears. Do not discount it though. Do not, for far more can be said in the silence of a well toned mind than from the tongues of a thousand jackals.

I awoke some hours later feeling warm and comfortable, apart from a dull ache in my neck. Never let it be said I had any sort of animosity toward sleeping on a sofa, but the body so often rebels the unusual positions we humans force upon them. And yet a warmth had been spread over my various limbs in the form of an afghan I had no recollection of ever seeing. The faded colors sang lullabies of years well past and gently tugged me back to sleep; accompanied by a deep, familiar snoring.

CHAPTER NINE

Were I to recite all the tales told to me upon my birth, I would paint a thousand years edging backward through Irish history. Stories of children led away by mischievous fairies or selkies shedding their seal skins upon barren shores. These were the works of old men; a fiction passed from age to age with nary a scratch or loosened syllable.

Then again, Keane, in his own right, was something of a fictitious character himself. He was a professor, and were that not enough, the breed of them that studied the inner workings of the brain. Surely that alone could place him in the same legend hood as America's unfortunate (and misshapen) obsession with leprechauns. If not quite that, then Lewis Carroll's mad hatter or cheshire cat. Even a less dangerous interpretation of Jekyll and Hyde. On land he was a gentleman, and indeed a gentle man. But once he stepped near the sea, he became captain. I had seen this on several occasions back in Devon. With navy-like precision, he would shove his little sailing ship out into the waves and skillfully maneuvered it about the towering cliffs.

But today we had no ships to sail, nor waves to watch, nor stones to skip. Today I abhorred the ocean.

"You've gone completely mad." I grumbled outward toward the man strutting about the shallow most waters. His shoes dangled round his neck and both trouser legs had been neatly rolled up to the knees. In many ways he looked rather like a crane. (An incredibly stupid crane, but a crane all the same.) His missing jacket, discarded on some "safe" rock, had left him free to push up his shirtsleeves before thrashing his strong, thin hands through the waters. "If it's a fish you want, we could go buy one. Seems a good deal more logical than taunting pneumonia." The latter portion was uttered more for my own benefit, but it traveled to my companion all the same.

"Save your indignation, Lawrence. You are free to go at any time you so wish." It was a lie. A very kind, sociable, acceptable lie.

Damn the man, he knew me all too well.

I sat on the grassy ledge to unlace my shoes. Soon the warm wool of my socks had been peeled away as well, along with my leather jacket and every inch of my patience. At the instant my bare skin touched water, I half wanted to yell shark, for a mighty jaw had clamped mightily to my innocent flesh. Great shoves of horrid cold brutally attacked the warmth of coursing blood; my one defense from such dastardly ice. My mind; however, was far more exposed to my companion's well clipped reticule that had only sharpened with the ocean's bite.

"For heaven's sake, stop floundering about and search."

"'Floundering' am I? Well then, *Professor*, what the devil are we looking for, and if you say fairies, I will personally drown you before boarding the first available passage back to England." Keane smiled that irritating, condescending smile of his before lightly tapping the greying hair of his right temple.

"Something round, hard, and infinitely blood covered."

"Oh, well that makes all the difference, doesn't it? And has it not occurred to you that this object may be well out to sea by now."

"It has, so you best hope we find it now, otherwise . . ." I wasn't certain what "otherwise" meant, but I most assuredly did not like that sparkle in his eye. Whoever said all boys become men obviously never met Keane when he had it in his head to try some newfangled gadget. Risking hypothermia and thousands of other fatalities, I searched the waters. After all, death might be an improvement over becoming a protege of Jules Verne.

Almost two hours later the ocean watched in victory as two weary soldiers slogged up onto the grass ledge. My teeth banged uncontrollably against each other and I could swear the ancestors of a blasted cold were creeping into my sinuses. Keane appeared entirely untouched by our morning adventure. Worse, the damn fool was grinning as knelt to do up his laces.

"I take it you'll be dragging me back here again?"

"My dear Lawrence, I hardly *dragged*—"

"Yes. Fine. Please at least tell me we will at least have time to warm up before coming back again." My companion said nothing but merely buttoned his overcoat. His fingers did not flinch as they wove the little circles through the adjoining fabric holes. Soon his thin hand was on my shoulder, along with a rich chuckle ringing softly in my ear.

"I make no promises."

I SAT CROSS-LEGGED on sands of woods with my Arabian tunic tucked securely round my shoulder and the final dregs of coffee sloshing idly in a simple mug. Keane himself had prudently chosen to perch on a stray cushion; looking rather like a maharaja and decidedly unlike the Irishman hidden beneath the heavy wool rugs. The only exception was his natural pallor topped with thick, blonde grey curls that might have been mistaken for red at some point in his youth. He seemed so thoughtful. So at peace. So . . . Keane. But his elegance and gentleness was a rarity in this family.

"Hello, Uncle Brendan." Michael swooped into the sitting room with a grand smile and handshake that barely caught Keane on his feet as the rugs slipped into a dismal pile on the floor. "Are you not well, Uncle? I hope you are not ill. Oh, and Joanna. How wonderful to see you. May I call you Joanna?" I was much too startled by the distinct sensation of a kiss upon my cheek to answer. Keane; however, was a professor equipped with an entire arsenal of words.

"And what has you in such a fine mood this morning, Michael? Come into money have you?"

"Och, how little you must think of me. Joanna, how do you put up with such a man. Surely you must have the patience of a saint."

"I assure you she has infinite patience, though considerably less for those who make a profession of doing nothing."

"Uncle Brendan, frowning does not flatter you. And to do so in the presence of such a beautiful young woman—" I know for a fact that I am not beautiful. Or at least not in the ways Michael seemed prone to admire. Even so, as a string of words reached my mouth, I was struck with a fear completely foreign to me; the ominous, overzealous, and inexcusable attack of a young man's lips.

"I must say, Mr. Keane, this is a change from when you nearly ran me down on the pavement."

"I can only hope you will forgive me for that dreadful accident, but I am sure you know what an frustrating old man my uncle can be. Speak of the devil, Uncle, would you mind terribly if I showed Joanna the stones. Any authoress should see them." Where the conversation had made me try to burrow myself further beneath the wool rugs, Keane had not salvaged his from the floor but merely sat in his shirtsleeves with a cup of coffee balanced on his knee. If he was such the model of ease, however, what were those extra carving marks on his face and where had all the blonde gone from his hair?

"You needn't ask me. She is capable of making up her own mind no matter what I say." My companion slowly climbed to his feet with the posture of a lord who stood before a firing squad. "Lawrence, you have nothing better to do this afternoon. Go see the stones with Michael."

"I will bring her back before supper."

"What the hell difference does that make? As I said, she is fully capable of her own decisions and living her own life." Keane grumbled fiercely; the blue of his eyes a frozen grey. Every inch of him reeked of dignity bordering violent explosion and I found myself torn between a bubbling anger and an inexplicable amount of pride at his ground words. And then the slate was washed with ice before falling into the turquoise depths of the ocean I curiously peered into a thousand times a day. But there was no energy in the cool waters; no life or sparkle that I so adored. There was nothing but that crisp voice leaping through air and grasping every bit of my attention. "Lawrence, the choice is entirely yours."

"You're sure you won't need my help with that little search and rescue mission? Fine then, I will go."

"Good. Have a grand time." Then there was the briefest glint of that familiar smile as he stepped toward the door; allowing his long, slender fingers to brush my hand as he passed. It was so brief. It was a mere instance that could have happened to anybody and entirely on accident.

But it didn't.

And then his clenched words hit a home run through my momentarily thick skull and everything fell into place in one shocking revelation.

Brendan Keane: the reverend professor of life's modern sciences; the man who walked through life with a commanding presence and resonant voice; the man respected for dozens of scientific manuscripts, short stories, and, in certain circles, a handful of fiction novels. The man. One of the great legends in our time.

Professor Brendan Keane.

Keane.

And he trusted me.

CHAPTER TEN

Where I had alway regarded Keane as a great and intelligent man, it was a pleasant surprise to find his nephew was not the complete idle buffoon I would have placed him for. Or at least, he had taken the time to review his history of the dirty slabs of earth wrenching out from the ground before me. There were thirteen I could clearly see, but marks and slated stumps convinced me of the ancient presence of four more. And then there was green; stretches and stretches of green smothered with snow and stopping only when it could go no further and dropped perilously into the ocean.

"It looks rather like the little town I used to make when I was a child." I laughed drily. It took more effort to laugh in a place like this. Deep mountains of green and white bowed over the scattered stones, as though all the world centered about this single place and the horrid fate it gave the ancestors who built it. A hand of ice dove down my spine. I jerked around toward Michael who was casually lounging atop a tower of grey boulders.

"They say the Druids built this place." He began slowly. "It served as an altar of sacrifice to their five gods." Michael slipped down from his high perch to join me at one of the taller stones. "Mercury was considered the highest of the gods, patron of the arts and so forth. Apollo drove away diseases. Minerva promoted handicrafts. Jupiter ruled the heavens. And Mars—"

"—controlled wars."

"You're familiar with mythology? But of course. My uncle. I don't know what you see in that old codger."

"What do you mean?"

"You have money, right? And lodgings of your own?" I nodded. "Then what the hell are you doing letting him drag you about with him?"

"He didn't drag me here. Ireland is in my blood." Michael scoffed at this, but it was without any ill feeling. Rather, it reflected more disbelief than anything.

"You're loyal to him. That's good. Every man should have someone loyal to him. Even if he is an elderly eccentric."

"Do you usually have so much snow here?" I forced the young man to look at the ground. To look at the white. To look away.

"No. Not often. But we have been suffering from a cold spell for many weeks now and it should clear up any day."

"I hope so. It's so much better green than covered in that grey mush."

"You really are a writer, aren't you?"

"I like to think so." A shimmering glimpse of teeth melted into a kind smile and the smooth pads of idle fingers bent down and grasped my hand. What an odd sensation it was, much like the kiss he inflicted on my cheek a few hours before. He held my hand as though it was of the most delegate china and his thumb running circles around the center of my palm.

"Have you ever seen the castle?" And then I was off; dragged by the hand across rocks and snow and grass and earth. Shoved above the slated cliffs and thrashing waves. Tossed about the stones that gnawed at my ankles. And though Michael took special care to maneuver me about such obstacles as a chess piece, I dared not close my eyes or risk missing a single inch of such a marvelously dangerous land. But then his hand came up and smothered my sight with darkness.

"No peeking, got it?" I slowly nodded before my feet were again being quickly led over winter's earth until at last Michael stopped and his hand fell away and with it all doubts I might have had that this sight was to be anything less than spectacular.

Unlike the stone circle, these grey slabs had been carefully mounted into walls, rooms, and towers before the giant of time trampled over the exquisite work. Winter had frozen ivy's fingers from the cracks between the stones, but perhaps the white made it all the better. All the less real. Truly it was a place detached from the world, much as the Druid's altar seemed all too fictional to have ever been a factor in human life. I opened my mouth to the world in resection.

"*'To him who had climbed the tower beyond time, consciously, and cast humanity, entered the earlier fountain.*' Robinson Jeffers wrote that line in The Tower Beyond Tragedy, though I never realized how right he was until this moment." Michael searched my face with his dark green eyes, and, when he could find no answer in the silence, he broke it.

"But what do you, Joanna Lawrence of the United States of America, think of it?"

"It's marvelous." Lightning flashed through the air in the form of two spotless hands clapping against the side of my face as two soft lips caught mine and branded them with a fiery heat. Fierce and hot.

HAD JUDAS NOT STRUNG himself from a tree before Jesus resurrected, he would have felt rather a great deal like I did when I came into the Keane household from the dimming streets a few hours later. Either that, or Judas had gotten lost on his way to Hell and entered the tomb made empty on Easter Sunday. Instead of an angel waiting for me; however, Thomas sat at the fire smoking a pipe with a bottle of whiskey at his side.

"Where's Keane?" The stem of his pipe stabbed upward through the air.

"In his bed."

"But it's not even six yet. God, he isn't ill is he?" That's just what I needed: Keane to be sleeping off a fever while I died being bored by his relations.

"Nothing that a bit of brains won't cure." Thomas' eyes flicked toward the ceiling. "That eejit brother of mine thought today of all days would be ideal for trying out that aqua-lung thingamajig. Never mind it's a bleeden invitation for the feckin' banshee." So that's what Keane had up his sleeve. Damn. Apart from an intimate dance with death, I might have enjoyed that. Ah, well, there were worse, more pressing matters pounding away at my head. There is never any respite for the wicked, and most certainly no pleasure in disloyalty to one's dearest friends.

As I opened the guest room door I was attacked by a sticky grey; dismal in every corner and yet somewhat a relief, for what can be seen in the light can just as easily hide in the dark.

Keane sat up in bed, propped with a small mountain of pillows and surrounded by soiled handkerchiefs. The more adventurous of the crumpled clothes had traveled onto the floor. A hot water bottle had been positioned carefully behind his neck, but it appeared to be doing little good. His face was red and raw, the wrinkled skin around his eyes puffy, and any trace of pomade in his wavy hair had been replaced by desertion among the ranks. If I were not so miserable, it might have been amusing to note the curl by his left ear trying desperately to salute a stray section hanging down on his forehead. But a sickness had inflicted my own stomach, which only lessened somewhat as I laid back on my bed.

"Lawrence, you missed a treat. The aqua-lung is a truly marvelous contraption. I wonder why I have not tried it before?"

"Perhaps for the very reason it took you several sniffles to get through those three sentences." Keane dared not say anything, but a thick cough erupted from his lungs, which I supposed was agreement enough. I glanced at the skillfully shaped metal laying idly on the bandstand beside a half drunk cup of herbal tea. "So, that's the weapon then? A revolver?"

"More specifically, an Enfield number two revolver. Go on then, I've already checked for fingerprints." The sheer weight of the object, matched with the red stains along the handle, screamed suspicion. Yet I was still surprised, and indeed startled, when I emptied six led capsules into my palm. A small victory upon such a horrid loss. A second cough followed the first and Keane shook his head violently to clear it.

"Now then, did you enjoy the stones?"

"I did. They were unlike anything I have ever seen. The castle was incredible as well. A writer's paradise."

"So Michael took you to the castle, did he?" Was it the buggered sinuses or anger that made Keane's voice scratch that way? "And what did you think of my nephew? Was he a good guide?"

"He was, though I am now thoroughly confused."

"Confused?" Damn my tongue. There you go, Lawrence. Dig yourself out of this one.

"Yes. I don't know which would be better to include in a novel. The stones of course have that air of mystery, but there is so much one can do with castle ruins. Ghosts, for instance. Ghosts are a good addition to any writer's portfolio." Keane made a sort of raspy grunt.

"Ghosts, my dear Lawrence, are merely overused entities to depict one's subconscious thoughts and desires." I flinched. Could he really see so clearly through my facade? I turned my face to the wall; the springs screaming with the motion. Every inch of my body wanted to sink into the fabric or flit away on a breeze. Ghosts indeed. That's what I wanted to be: a ghost. However, as with so many other idle wishes, it was not to be. Or at least, not in the presence of one Professor Brendan Keane. There was the general discomfort of springs (along with several other more colorful syllables) as he shifted his long form about that he was not only able to look fully at me, but he might bound for an attack at any given moment. What a fool I was to glance back at him, but how could I not? It made no difference. His eyes were slate without etching: unreadable.

"Tell me truthfully, Lawrence," He began; his normally rich voice a tad raspy from illness. "Did you enjoy Michael's company?"

"Yes . . . Yes, I did." There was nothing then. Nothing but the swift passing of time through the echoes of silence. Several times I wished to shatter the thickness of the air and feel the obstructive silence crumble between my frozen fingers, but each time I gathered courage enough to look at my companion, my friend, the man I felt sure I had betrayed, he lay motionless with his head tilted back upon the mountain of pillows. And, though his eyes were closed and did not flinch, I was certain of one thing.

He would not snore.

BEYOND THE SNIFFLES and coughing that racked his chest through the night, Keane did indeed arise the next day in as high of spirits as any struck Irishman may accomplish. Though I myself was not specifically Irish in birth, it was still so much a part of me it did not take much effort to recognize it in others. He smiled politely when necessary, bantered constantly with his brother, and remained just as I had always known him: Professor Brendan Keane. On the surface.

Had I not known him for so many years, I might not have caught that falter of gentlemanly grace when Michael came through the kitchen door at breakfast. It was just a slight slip; causing a ripple in his teacup, rather than a spill. But it was enough that there were a few blood drawn moments set between the snap of the door latch to Thomas' gritty voice saving Catherine's china from falling from Keane's fingers to the floor.

"Jesus, Mary, and Joseph, how'd you do that?"

"This?" The young man fingered the darkly colored skin thickly encircling his left eye. It was a miracle the lids hadn't swollen shut by the sheer size of the thing. "Won it inside the ring last night. I never thought that big bloke would be fast enough to land one, but clearly I was mistaken." Thomas chuckled slightly as he slapped his son's shoulder.

"Bren here knows a lot about that one. Don't you?" Keane shifted slightly in his chair, but that was more than sufficient admittance for Michael to painfully raise an eyebrow.

"Is that so, Uncle? You fought in the rings?"

"That was some time ago. Boxing is a young man's sport, and I am no longer a young man." This from the man who could master any terrain, return life to shell-shocked soldiers, and hold his drink better than a man ten times younger and a hundred times stronger (even if he did lose the battle every once in a while). This from the man I held in the greatest adoration. This from the man I betrayed.

"Would you care for some breakfast, Michael? It's still warm."

"No, Ma, but thanks all the same." The young man shifted his gaze from the plate of kippers to the door back to me. How odd it is to be looked upon with the same social standing as a cooked fish, but then, I did share one thing with that breakfast morsel. We both bore the distinct smell of red herring.

CHAPTER ELEVEN

The solicitor took his place before me; his hands fiddling with the knot of his tie while the jury and judge resided in the other room. Nervous as the young man was, he scarcely waited for the door to be closed before strangled words began bubbling from his mouth.

"I really am sorry about the whole thing. I shouldn't have—that is—I didn't think—" Bloody Hell he didn't. And even if he was telling the truth, he would most certainly think from now on. At least he might if his mouth stopped moving. " . . . You had every right to hit me—"

"Damn right I did! What did you think I was? Some woman to be putty enough to kiss whenever you damn well please?"

"I didn't know—"

"—Know what? That I would give you a shiner? Well I did, and unless you want another one—in a place I am too much of a lady to mention—you had best be on your way." Suddenly he stopped fidgeting with that infernal tie of his and began to do one of the most idiotic things the male sex ever invented to solve a situation. A slim grin slipped onto his youthful, albeit somewhat battered, face.

"God, you're beautiful when you're angry." I cocked a clenched fist back, but he held up his open palm. "I'll be on my way, but just know that, whatever else I may be, I am not a liar. I really am quite fond of you, Joanna Lawrence. Even if we could only be friends, that would be enough for me. Good-bye." I was vaguely aware that, within the murk of his words, Michael left and Keane had replaced his position: a cup of tea balanced between his hands. He said nothing. Very sarcastically.

"I'm going back to England." I announced at last. What a joy it was to see that rare look of pure shock flit across his long features and the drop of now tepid tea sloshing from its cup and onto his shoes. It was a great victory: like a knife being stabbed between your ribs before ripping downward through the internal organs. Keane must have felt my blood spurt outward as well, for his posture grew rigid and those soft, gentle eyes instantly became a book to a blind man. Even his voice, stripped clean of the ills of the past night, bore no more expression than that of a record spinning monotonously on a phonograph.

"How long?" He asked. How long. Like I bloody well cared now. He was the professor. He was the one who always had the answers. It was his interest, not mine, that so often drew us into these problems of untimely deaths stained with guilty blood. It was his—all of it—and, for once in my life, I felt that I had slipped away from my place on Mercury and was flung away into Pluto's tedious orbit. I was small and insignificant against the sun. Who knows, perhaps in a few decades, the very people who discovered my place among the debris would deny my existence. Or worse, claim that I am not worthy to belong with the other eight planets.

But how could I say this? How could I pour my thoughts out before the sun and risk them being burned in his reticule. Therefore, I answered with one of the most intelligent phrases I could muster and hurled it directly into his orbit so it would wander round and round his head before absorbing into his ears.

"I don't know."

PART THREE

Being entirely honest with oneself is a good exercise.
Sigmund Freud

CHAPTER TWELVE

Whoever spent the past December dreaming of a white Christmas to resurrect some childhood nostalgia would have been mortified to know the godforsaken words forming between my ears. The white fluff tumbling from the sky could be a grand thing... when it was convenient. By the late hour I stumbled into Keane's house in Devon; however, "snow" was a word just as unsociable as the long string of forbidden curses that could put any mother superior in her coffin before you reached the nonexistent second syllable. My insides were just as cold as the outsides and every inch screamed for an immediate remedy. Boots still frozen to my ankles, I staggered into the foyer, down the hall, and into the kitchen. Tea. Damn it, that's what I needed: a hot cup of tea. I flung on the lights, waited a few moments for my eyes to stop burning, then scrambled about the cupboards for the dark green tin. Keane was a great stickler on his tea, as he had proven within my first week of our acquaintance. There are a few things one finds infinitely difficult to believe until one sees it. A grown man throwing a cup of tea through a window pane was one of them. No, English tea was out of the question in his house. It had to be brought in from Cork; the same dark and aromatic blend used by his family for many years.

I popped off the painted lid and clumsily poured some leaves into the metal strainer. Some, of course, was too much, but few would be not enough. It didn't matter though, for, after mucking about with a few knobs on the stove, I turned them all off and smacked the damn thing. I was never well placed in a kitchen, and the only thing I could possibly cook in my exhausted state, would be my body dead with asphyxiation. Turned tails I did and inched my way further down the hall toward a pair of enormous, oak doors. My feet led my eyes through the dim shadows until at last they faltered and flung me into the arms of a great leather. The cool surface still bore the slightest scent of tobacco stirred evenly with hair pomade and cologne. I pressed my nose to the chair's high backing and breathed; for no greater remedy is there on earth than to breathe.

THE THICK, COMPELLING smells of frying bacon quickly overpowered the lingering aroma captured within the leather of the armchair. Both my legs had become entirely too numb for my liking and the tops of my boots had pressed into my ankles until little angry lines dug along my flesh. I flexed my fingers experimentally while stretching my legs out in front of me. Strange, I hadn't noticed that much mud on my trousers last night. Long, thick splotches coated the heavy fabric; caked too well into the fibers to brush away with a mere hand. Rather like the house I had entered so late—or was it early—last night.

Keane's grey, pebble-peppered, two-story house had dotted the Devon landscape for the past hundred and fifty years or so, and was thereby one of the few pillars left of times gone by that were not being rebuilt from rubble. The walls of each hall and room had been skillfully papered in rather unusual patterns that wavered between brown and green; yet, as unappealing as it may sound, it was rather pleasant to look at. Stretches of hardwood flooring had been covered in tan rugs and a handful of tasteful paintings greeted you at every turn. Mrs. McCarthy's touch could often be seen stretching from her kitchen in the form of vases and other decor of equal femininity. I waited for the day when Keane at last followed through with his billowing threats and smashed some of the more floral pieces into the ground, but, deep down, I knew that day was more likely to come from the past rather than some future spectacle.

 I stretched again and peered around me as I had most every time I entered the study. It was the one room of the house Mrs. McCarthy could not touch, for indeed, in all the time I had known the house, this room was most entirely Keane's. The walls had been papered in a marbling of faded oranges, greens, and browns; creating an effect that absolutely reeked of masculinity. Bookcases lined whatever wall space that was not occupied by mismatched frames or tall windows with white painted rims. A sort of balcony had also been added to supply an even greater amount of shelf space. Were one to ascend on the spiral staircase, one might even mistake the enormous selection of volumes for heaven. An enormous fireplace held council over an assortment of armchairs and such at the far end of the room. Then there was, of course, a writing desk, bowls of cigarettes, stray matchboxes, and intricate model sailing ships. In the corner nearest myself sat a radio and phonograph, along with several crates of records varying from Keane's more classical tastes to my meagre collection of Bing Crosby and Red Nichols. Unlike most every other part of the house, there were no paintings in this room; only faded photographs depicting colorless figures forever entrapped in stiff positions that made my sore shoulders ache.

 My mind was raked away once more by another strong waft of bacon, along with the promises of eggs and—tea! I was dragged to my feet by my throat and stumbled tiredly onward until I reached the sanctity of the kitchen. As the study was entirely Keane's, the kitchen was Mrs. McCarthy's domain to be dealt with as much tough mercy as a five star general. And a general she was. Her short, silver hair was always perfectly curled and made a neat nest for a modest hat, of which she must have hundreds. Her plum colored skirt suit was worn with nary a crease from the closet, nor smudge from the wooden spoon in her hand. A weapon more lethal than a gun.

"Jesus, Mary, and Joseph, get those filthy boots off your feet this instant! I just finished cleaning the footprints I found when I came in, as well as the mess you made in my kitchen here. Tea leaves all over the table and dishes you never used. If I weren't a good Christian woman I would—" In two long strides I wrapped the housekeeper in a quick embrace that left her scarcely retaining what frustration I seemed to cause every day without fail. But it always ended the same way. "—Well, that's alright then. Though mind you don't do it again." At least, for a while anyway.

"I promise. Now, is that breakfast I smell?"

CHAPTER THIRTEEN

"I should arrest youse for withholding evidence." The young Sergeant Walsh spat across the still cluttered desk. "If it is evidence, that is. For all I know you could have gone out and bashed a pig with the feckin thing, gombeen that you are, so." Keane pinched the bridge of his nose. It had been a good many years since he had been accused of that particular term and, while it was not perhaps one of the more offending insults, the lad had sported a bent nose through the rest of their school days. Keane doubted the same tactic would work here, though the tenacious youth damn well needed it.

"I assure you it is one of the murder weapons." The Garda glanced down at the revolver set before him then back up at the professor's set expression.

"But there were no bullets found in either body. And the lass, she had water in her lungs. You saw the reports."

"Indeed I did. I also found finger-like bruises along the throat and a crushing blow in her head." Keane stabbed a slender finger toward the offending object. "That is the attacker's chosen weapon."

"But, if you or I were to hit something—anything—with that revolver it would—"

WHAM!

Before he could finish, the professor had grabbed the gun by the barrel and slammed it handle first into the edge of the desk; knocking away a chip of wood from the surface. But, much to Sergeant Walsh's utter shock, Keane stood casually before him without a spent bullet anywhere near his person. Rather, the grey-haired devil was grinning wildly from ear to ear. The sergeant gasped like a child in the presence of a magician, then stuttered for a moment before the engine in his mouth was sufficiently stoked.

"How . . . You took out the bullets! That's what you did! Sure I knew you'd be a tricky one, but—" Keane, revolver still in hand, dumped six led capsules onto an unruly stack of paperwork. Sergeant Walsh stumbled backward into his chair. "You're mad, you are. Mad as a hatter, so."

"Sergeant, you know something about firearms, don't you?"

"Does a donkey know how to shit?" Keane's nose wrinkled slightly.

"Indeed, well then you might recognize the significance of this." A piece of metal was thrust between the young man's eyes to the point the odor of wet metal and gun oil were not only probable but unavoidable. He took the shard into his trembling hands.

"Sure, it's a firing pin, so it is. Filled down, right there before me very eyes. Bejeezus, I'm a feckin eejit, so I am." Keane thrust the words playing on his lips to the back of his brain and leaned forward until he towered over the Garda.

"You see then it was murder?"

"See it? How could I've missed it? Bejeezus, I'm a feckin—"

"Be that as it may, I assume you will now take the necessary steps to properly investigate?" Sergeant Walsh stood and outstretched a wiry hand.

"That I will, Sir. That I will."

A man who loses his leg in battle is so full of adrenaline that he often does not realize its loss until he reaches down to ease away the pain. No doubt Shaw's Henry Higgins felt much the same when Eliza went off with that Freddy character. Keane could sympathize with the man, not for his bubbling romanticisms, but rather for the loss of a second party with whom ideas may be traded equally and not buzzing about his brain like a nest of wild hornets. Lawrence was never so prone to female emotions as she was to that vicious temper of hers, and yet, he could not help but believe—as a man of psychiatry—that there was some emotion lying at the bottom of all this. Keane himself had seen the unfortunate lad, even felt the unnatural rubber of the corpse as it bounced against the cart, but it had been Lawrence who found the mound of mutilated flesh. It had been she to first look into the dull, foggy eyes of death. It had been she who accepted one of his cigarettes and finished it as one who had gone through the motions a thousand times before. It was she. And he damn well knew it.

Keane adjusted his course toward the nearest pub just as a cold drizzle began to drip from the sky. The city had changed somewhat since he had last visited. (What was that? Twenty—no—thirty years ago. God, was he really getting that old?) The sweet shop was no longer there, and the chemist's had moved across the street. What was once mainly carts had fallen prey to a brigade of automobiles rambling up and down with noisy motors and mud stained fenders. Keane glanced toward a pile of empty fruit crates where a scraggly, bearded man was sprawled. His patch-covered limbs wove through the thin gaps between the wood and the tarp he had used as a blanket had fallen away to expose one of his sleeves pinned up where his arm should have been. In his one hand was a dirty brown bag with the green neck of a bottle peeking out at the top. He lay stupefied; completely oblivious to the world rotating around him. Modern appliances and motorcars meant nothing, for, while the rest of the world may carry on, some things are forever incapable of change. There would always be two sides to every street and railroad. There would always be a yesterday more sure than tomorrow. And, Keane thought, there would always be a mysterious illness that caused immediate blindness whenever a person came near someone decidedly unlike themselves. Keane rummaged around his pockets and slipped a handful of coins into the man's only pocket held together with more than a few wisps of thread. It would, he hoped, be enough for a day's worth of hot meals. If the man spent it on liquor—oh, well, at least he would have a few good drinks to keep out the cold and a cigarette or two among friends. A man should have friends.

IT WASN'T THE SAME pub he knew in his youth, but, after a few fine pints, Keane found it satisfactory enough. The walls were of aged oak and the low hum of conversation mingled pleasantly with the drink. Where the streets grew colder day by day, the pub was warm enough to permit tiny beads of sweat to form at the edge of his collar. A tipsy ancient man in more patches than clothing played a whistle in the corner; held up only by a strong succession of pints from enthralled regulars. At first the high screeching had grated upon his ears, but, somewhere into his third stout the noise slipped from bearable to enjoyable. Keane rapped his fingertips against the side of his glass in time with the musician's erratic song.

"Excuse me, sir. A wee word?" The voice at the professor's shoulder was low and would have been commanding had it not been lubricated by the stale stench of a dozen kinds of ale.

Before Keane could turn about in the old wooden chair, the man plopped down at the other end of the short table. He looked a good deal more sober since the last time they met, though even that was not much of an improvement. The man's massive size caused the stool to groan and whimper with each raspy breath that rattled the brigade of crumbs peppering his white, unkempt beard. Was it the light or did the man's skin look a bit yellow?

Keane motioned to the bar.

"May I?"

"God bless you, sir." The man slurred as he drained the last of the copper liquid. The loud burp that followed was enough to make the tendons in Keane's neck flinch. "Did ya' know it's a crime for a man to go thirsty?" The man was hardly dying of thirst, the professor thought. Drowning, perhaps, by certainly not dying. A round of stout was brought to the table. The man scarcely was able to mutter his thanks before draining a third of it in a single draw. Then he looked up at Professor Keane as though it was the first time he realized the man existed.

"Have we met b'fore, sir?"

"Once," Keane answered evenly. "though you were rather worse for wear at the time." The man blinked a few times. Suddenly his meaty hand slammed onto the table, sloshing the froth over the glass' edge.

"Sure, I remember now. You was asking about that poor lad who was cut up. Heard about the ma, so. Sorry lot."

"You knew her then?"

"Sure . . . Oh, sure. She was a pretty thing. A real looker when she dressed right, if you get me drift." However obtuse might have been mentally, it also pertained to most every portion of the man's physical state except for the elbow suddenly jammed into Keane's side. "Too bad ol' Jimmy there had to let 'er off the pay." The man leaned forward onto the table until the reeking stench of months of perspiration and drink burned the professor's eyes. "On normal occasions I wouldn't be telling no one about that, sir. State secret like, so it is. But I saw yer with that trousered lass—"

"—Did you really?" Keane could feel his fingers clench into a fist beneath the table until the fingernails were in serious danger of penetrating flesh. No, he would not strike. It was undignified. What was it his father had always said?

Dignity. Dignity always.

Bloody hell. What had dignity ever done but locked Bridget in a cell until her skin was near transparent against the cold, grey, stones. What made her so different from them: them and their drinking and dark secrets hidden away beneath a casket of lies? What had built that steel door between her and them? Wasn't everyone just a little insane? The world would be terribly dull if there were no groups, no social dynamic to make the world spin and no static to enjoy. After all, was there really anything wrong with imagination? Weren't they all taught in their youth the world rotated on an imaginary axis? Lawrence used imagination for her writing. What was so wrong if Bridget did the same? What was so wrong?

"Nothing wrong with having a bit of fun, sir." The man's slippery syllables continued. "Nothing wrong at all, even if they aren't always well built. You never married, sir?"

"Never."

"See, now there's nothing the matter with that. Tried it myself once. Didn't like it—the Missus started getting too virtuous—so I got out fast as me old legs could take me. Nothing the matter with nothing, except that lass' boy."

"The one who was murdered?" The man nodded and spilled a swallow of amber liquid down his shirt. By the various other stains; however, it made little difference.

"So they're calling it murder now, eh? Sure, that's the one. Scrappy little lad—don't think I don't feel sorry for the gobsheen, cause I damn well do—just hard to see the Almighty shedding too many tears over that little piece of gobshite." Keane's fist began to shake beneath the table.

"He seemed like a fine child when I met him."

"Sure, I'm not saying he was evil or nothing, so. Just that he was missing a few things up here." The man pressed a well padded finger to his forehead. "Eejit like, if you get me. Had half the bar out searching for him half a dozen times only to find him in the forest down a ways. Do'ya know what he said when we found him? 'Out chasing fairies', he said. Don't know about you, sir, but I know there ain't no goddamn fairies round here." Keane took a long draw of stout. He was beginning to sympathize with Lawrence's impatience with the mythical creatures.

"I believe you did tell me a few days ago." The man blinked.

"Did I? Well it's worth saying again. Did I tell you of the men? No? The gobshite would start howling for nothing, crying that he saw some group of men with dark hoods. Strange thing was no one else was even close to the lad, 'cept his mother. She wouldn't let him leave her side for nothing."

"Dark hoods, you say?"

"Sure, that's right. And tattoos and scarred faces. Sure, just like you see in those American movies. Almost like—och, what's the name . . . Boris Karloff? Sure, that's it. Boris Karloff." The man was so pleased with remembering the English actor's name he appeared utterly oblivious to the waterfall of amber pouring from his glass. Keane rose, slid a silver coin across the battered table, and reached for his overcoat. The man took his coin in his thick palm.

"You're a real gentleman, sir." He slurred. Keane scoffed and reached for his cigarette case. A real gentleman his arse.

CHAPTER FOURTEEN

A gentleman. A breed there would never be in plenty. There were characteristics shared by those who came very close, but often enough those virtues were quickly spoiled by some scandal lurking beneath a history of "good breeding". What was breeding anyway but the assurance you had a great-great-grandfather two times removed from some other important gentleman who decided to give his distant relation a title for rescuing his favorite cat.

Such was Lord Billington.

To look at him was to know of all his intelligence, which was severely lacking. His short, spindly frame ballooned out at the midsection and his face bore very little color save a very red nose.

"Good morning, Miss Lawrence. Fine day, isn't it?" Three days. Three cold days and I had not managed to avoid the little man for a single one of them. Keane should receive sainthood for living in a radius less than five miles from the lord's estate, but, considering the world's fortune in having not been acquainted to Billington, the honor was—at best—unlikely.

"It is indeed, my lord." My lord indeed. 'Buffoon' would be a far more logical title. He quickened his pace and tried to keep time with me, dragging his fat dog behind him. Though I suppose one could do little with the dog otherwise. It would have been one of the most miserable of hunting hounds, for it was so heavy its belly sagged to the ground no matter the position. Much like his master, come to think of it.

"And where is the professor on this fine day? I do hope he isn't ill."

"No, sir. He is in Ireland with his family." The titled monkey huffed obnoxiously in my ear. (Whether it was from distaste, surprise, or the physical exercise I was not entirely certain, but I suspected the latter.)

"Family? I didn't know the professor was human enough to have a family. Strange one, he is—like a machine—utterly inhumane—but what you and he do is no one's business but your own."

"What we do?"

"Yes. That psycho—psycho-alianithi—"

"—psychoanalysis."

"It makes no difference what you call it. It's the devil's work all the same. Take that one German for instance. Simon Freud—"

"—*Sigmund* Freud" God, it was like trying to have an intelligent conversation with an overgrown infant. "And he was Austrian, not German." The man shrugged, exposing the unseemly tightness of the clothes at his middle.

"German, Austrian, doesn't matter. He ended his own life, didn't he? Just like Hitler." I held my tongue. It would make little difference to this poor specimen of a man that Freud had committed suicide to escape the pain of a cancerous tumor. Hitler did so when his maddened dreams of complete dictatorship crumbled.

"They were two very different people." I stated simply as the obese man mopped his forehead with a crumpled handkerchief, only for the sweat to mix with the grease in his black hair.

"Ought to have been locked up from the beginning. The whole lot of them."

"What ever for? Freud may have been a grumpy old man, but he did make some advances in psychology people will be studying for decades to come."

"But he was a madman, and they don't belong anywhere near us. Wouldn't you agree, Miss Lawrence?"

"BILLINGTON IS A BLOODY imbecile! A leach on the ass of society!" I flung my jacket into the closet with a muffled thump and very nearly bulldozed into Mrs. McCarthy in the process.

"Jezus, Mary, and Joseph! I just cleaned those rugs!" I mumbled an apology and kicked off my mud coated boots, which Mrs. McCarthy quickly swept into her arms. "Thank you. Now, I have a fresh batch of muffins in the kitchen . . . "

A few minutes later I burst into the study with a plate of Mrs. McCarthy's baked goods and King Lear tucked comfortably under my arm. Between the leather armchair and the sofa, I avoided the first and set both plate and book on the latter before striding over to the phonograph. It is true I did have my own lodgings, a much smaller cottage ten miles down that I inherited from some obscure relation, but my home had always been in this place. My house was really just a luxury.

I slipped a Glenn Miller record onto the machine and carefully dropped the needle. Deep, quick blares erupted from the funnel. Keane could enjoy all the classical music he wanted, but this, this was life itself swirling about in thick circles of the purest energy humanity had ever known. What could be made beautiful with a selection of fine strings was made lively by a replacement of a brass ensemble. Eventually the needle ran out of music. Rather than simply changing the record to the other side; however, I replaced it completely with what I knew to be a rather soothing collection of Beethoven. As soon as the briefest droplets of violins spewed outward into the room, I settled back on the sofa and set the book in my lap. It was among the few Shakespeare plays I had yet to read. Perhaps it was in my ignorance that made Keane all the more incline to draw quotes from the musty pages. I ran my hand gently over the worn cover. It had not been on the shelf with the hundreds of others. It had not even been in the study. I had discovered the copy quite unintentionally the evening before when going into Keane's private office: a small room in which only a small desk, telephone, and typewriter could be found. It had been lying silently atop a stack of fresh writing paper. I gently lifted the front cover and gasped.

To my most treasured brother,

Trí ní is deacair a thuiscint; intleacht na mban, obair na mbeach, teacht agus imeacht na taoide.

With all my love,
Bridget
8th April 1918

I swallowed hard. The carefully penned script was simple against the yellowing page, and yet . . . and yet, there was so much more that remained unsaid within these papered walls. My knowledge of the Irish language was much too lacking to decipher the spirals of ink, but the gaiety of each metallic stroke warned of some jest that would most assuredly cause the owner to smile and run his calloused hand gently over the spider's ballet. I shut the cover reverently and stared at the cover. 1918. She must have been about 18 then. An adult in every right. But she had no rights. Not really, anyway. Rights, like dignity, were immediately stripped the moment one stepped behind that steel door. It was a fate far worse than death. A fate so foul with shame a mother would rather forget her daughter in a pine box than love her through metal bars. Even Thomas had followed along in the facade of her death; seemingly immune to the guilt and pain of losing a relation. Keane seemed the only one to mourn in the light and weep in the darkness. It was he who rebuked—even blamed his brother for the hell in which Brigit was forced to travel. I would not have been surprised if Keane had visited her more than once, however painful it may be. I myself had seen the virtues and sins of modern medicines. I had seen men cured of pneumonia: the smiles and detached words of thanks. But there was an evil claimed necessary by the blind and merciful for the heartless.

My ears rang with the terrified screams muffled with opium injected into her fragile veins. Her face, gaunt and sharp, sucked at her glazed eyes while shards of crudely cut straw remained matted to her scalp with sweat and filth. The rags wrapped around her hid nothing but a skeleton and just as dead. Dead as ash and just as bitter.

CHAPTER FIFTEEN

One step and he was as dead to the world as it was to him. One flinch and it would end. One single slip.

It was absurdly simple how one could throw their body over the cliff and feel discomfort for the briefest moment before smashing against the merciless rocks below. Dead.

"Did you lose something?" Keane spun around and allowed a generous smile to play across his face.

"Hello, Michael. No, but if you see some marbles lying about, they're mine." The young nephew grinned sheepishly.

"I'm glad to see you in such high spirits. After the other day—well—let's just say we haven't seemed to get off on the right foot since you came back."

"A lot of years have passed. But I agree. Apart from that conversation over a week ago, we haven't really had the chance to have a proper conversation." Michael nodded toward the sudden drop of the landscape into the frothy waters below.

"And we won't if you throw yourself into that." Keane chuckled dryly.

"Hardly. I may not be a young man anymore, but nor am I desperate to meet the Almighty any time in the near future." Michael smiled then quickly regained a sobriety unusual for a young man.

"Joanna told me you were helping with that mother and son case. Anything I can do?"

"Thank you, but right now I don't need much more than a stiff drink." Keane's stomach growled audibly through his coat.

"And something to eat too, by the sounds of it. Ma said you rushed out without your supper."

"It's nothing that a visit to the Duck won't cure . . . later." Keane gave a long, wistful glance back toward the precipice. "Michael, have you ever had that feeling that the answer to all your problems is staring you back in the face?"

"Sure I have. Usually it reveals itself after a good jar or two." The older of the two men grunted before allowing the edge of his lips to creep upward into the softest beginnings of a smile.

"What butter or whiskey does not cure—"

"—Cannot be cured. To the Duck then?"

The chill of the wind had again turned cold. Far too cold for the winters Keane remembered. Or perhaps he had forgotten. It had been quite a long time since he had last set foot in this place for more than a few hours—a day at most. Last he had seen of Michael was before the war, and he was still a boy then; not the towering young man that had swept in and taken Lawrence to the great county sights. All in all, he rather liked the young man. He was, admittedly, well blessed with that modernistic handsome that girls seemed to admire. As they walked, Keane noticed Michael's fingers reaching up every so often to trace the light outline of what once had been a vicious bruise.

"Lawrence did that, didn't she?" The nephew stopped and stared at his uncle, who chuckled. "Don't look so surprised, lad. To her it's as common as a handshake." Michael watched his boots slip along the paths of mud and ice.

"I didn't mean to offend her, so I didn't."

"Michael, if I were a betting man, I would give you odds that you didn't offend anyone. You might have bruised—pun intended—you pride a bit, but other than that," Keane shrugged. "Lawrence is a special kind of young woman, not the sort you can go around kissing just as you please—let me finish, man—You can't catch her as you would a bird. You must respect her enough to let her fly free and trust that, in the end, she will find her way back home by herself when she's good and ready."

"Like Bridget?" The professor suddenly lost his footing and would have tumbled down the hill if he hadn't recovered enough to right himself.

"I—I wasn't aware you knew about her." Michael turned his nose toward a particularly fascinating blade of grass.

"Da kept saying she was dead, but I knew he was lying—I'll be damned if I knew why I thought it. So I did a little digging and found her files tucked away in the Richland up in Dublin. As of five years ago she was still alive up there and being taken care of by a Doctor McCladah.

When I asked me Da about that bit, the whole story came pouring out like Jonah from the whale's mouth. Everything. Her delusions. Her wit. Her intelligence in spite of it all. He said she was more like you than anything; followed in your wake like a puppy. And she clutched her arms around that doll you gave her even when the men from the asylum—"

"—Not bad for a man who studies anthropology." Keane choked out. His throat was a desert and his tongue had been replaced by a heavy slab of cotton. The insides of his eyelids prickled like needles stabbing into his brain. God, he needed a drink. Something infinitely strong and several jars of it if necessary. In England he had managed—not to forget—but to quell that overpowering, sharp guilt that had first struck him when he returned from Dublin to find Bridget gone. He should have done something more to protect her. He should have known somehow of the plot hidden behind him. But, now that he had returned to his homeland, all those raw emotions stabbed through him as a sharp knife: thrashing deep lines into his flesh until he was not but a dead shell falling... falling... falling...

"H'llo, Uncle? Thought I lost you for a moment. Anyway, we're here. Go right on and find a pew. I've got to see a man about a wee dog."

Keane watched the young man—his nephew, by God—slip through the regiments of men in cloth caps and heavy wool coats. A nice glass of Middleton's in hand, he found a place in the corner and settled himself wearily into the chair. Either he was getting older or the day was getting longer. He wasn't quite certain which was which. Fortunately, a long drawl of whiskey—along with a good smoke—tended to clear his mind. And yet his mind seemed most desperate not to be cleared.

"Brendan, you old fart. How the hell are you?" A booming voice echoed behind him as a strong hand smacked him brutally between the shoulders. Keane jumped to his feet and spun around with a boyish grin.

"Fingal? Fingal Francis O'Malley. By God, it's good to see you. It's been too long."

"You're damn right it has. Look at you—" The large man pushed Keane back a bit while still keeping a bear-like hand on his shoulder. "That Mrs. McCarthy sure as hell's been doing a good job. Looks like you've got some extra meat on your bones." The professor chuckled and eyed the soft bulge of Fingal's waist line.

"You've put on a few too, I see."

"Aye, my damn housekeeper, God bless her, keeps trying to serve me bloody salads 'stead of a good, hearty meal."

"Well have a pew, O'Malley, and let me buy you a drink. Or should I be calling you Doctor O'Malley? I heard about your graduation a few weeks after I left for England. Good for you." The large man smiled and pulled out a worn wooden pipe.

"S'pose I should be saying the same to you, you great bollox. Professor, eh? Your nose always was an inch higher than your face. Remember the time you just about tripped over yourself when it came to a certain Miss Dedrie Barkley? You were more disorientated than the local drunk." Keane laughed into his whiskey.

"Deidre? How could I forget? No sooner did you drag me away from her than you started following her like a damn puppy." Fingal downed a good swallow of his pint.

"Don't be spreading that one around. My Madeline would have me out of the house within the hour."

"How is that darling wife of yours?"

"All the better if she heard you saying that. Keep up that blarney of yours and I'll have to challenge you to a duel to the death. You're still a bachelor, aren't you? Lucky lummox. No one breathing down your collar every time you need a wee drink to keep the throat from going dry." The doctor took another large swig from the frothy glass. Little had changed about him in the last thirty years. His hair, though perhaps a bit grey here and there, remained a dark, overgrown shag that covered the tops of his cauliflower ears and touched a set of bushy eyebrows positioned over dark brown eyes. His color had always been vivid; a pink, ruddy hue from all those days spent on the rugby team. Fingal sat back in his chair and released a blue haze of pipe smoke.

"Look at us, Brendan," He chuckled. "Two old men. Where have the last thirty years gone?" Keane was about to reply when Michael returned with a small glass cradled between his hands.

"Fingal, meet my nephew, Michael Keane. Michael, this is an old friend of mine, Doctor Fingal O'Malley" The doctor stood and shook the young man's hand, which was almost tiny in comparison.

"I take it you're a university man, Michael."

"Yes, sir. I began studying anthropology three years ago, right after my discharge from the military." Fingal nodded solemnly.

"A lot of good men were lost in the war. Both of them."

"Aye." Keane agreed. "Too many." All three took a drink in unison; a silent toast between two who suffered the first war and one fresh from the second. The moment only ended with the angry roar of a motor outside. Keane glanced quickly behind him before returning his attention back to his comrades.

"If Lawrence were here, we'd be hearing about every fathomable fact possibly known about that blasted contraption. She's the regular encyclopedia of information when it comes to such things." Fingal O'Malley slyly grinned.

"So it's a she, is it? Thinking of ending that solitary life of your's, Brendan?" Keane chuckled.

"I think not. All she knows about the Great War was taught to her in history books. But, by God, her intelligence is astounding."

"Not to mention her fists." Michael added, touching the still slightly colored skin at his eye. Fingal's eyebrows shot up only seconds before the pub echoed with great guffaws of laughter.

"She did that to you? Sweet jeezus, you did find a real treasure. Whenever my Madeline gets her knickers in a twist, she takes it out on the rugs. I'll be having to buy new ones soon."

"Mrs. McCarthy's much the same, though the only thing more lethal than that woman's mighty tongue is her rolling pin. A damn sight more dangerous than those raps we used to get for misbehaving during mass. Remember that one, Fingal?"

"My knuckles sting just from thinking about it. I also remember that you were seriously considering becoming a man of the cloth at one time." Michael nearly choked on his whiskey.

"Uncle? You wanted to be a priest?" Keane's eyes twinkled mischievously.

"At one time, yes. I thought it would be rather fun to be the one boring other people to tears. Later, after I graduated as a psychologist, I realized it was a bloody good thing I didn't. American politicians are far better at lulling someone to sleep, and they do it without taking a vow of celibacy." At this Keane's young nephew did sputter on the amber liquor, for his uncle's face bore that distinct, youthful smile that made him seriously question whether or not he was quite serious. It is often difficult to imagine a relative taking part in such intimate acts made all the more scandalous when not supported by that seal of approval made frivolous by white lace gowns and champagne.

Doctor O'Malley wagged his head with a deep chuckle.

"And, while we're investigating your many vices, how's that smoking habit of yours? Do you still smoke—what was it—five packs a day?"

"About that amount, yes."

"I should be warning you that doctor's think smoking's bad for your health. That's what the researchers are starting to say, anyway. But I don't think you'd pay it any mind." Keane slipped out one of the thin cylinders, pressed it between his lips, and lit the paper end.

"You underestimate me then, Fingal. I've tried to quit twice already and it damn near killed me. I'd rather die from something I enjoy than wither away like some daft old tea-totaler."

"Heaven forbid." The doctor muttered sarcastically. "I suppose you're referring to Old Willow Winston, son of a gobshite that he is."

"Old Willow Winston?" Michael asked. The two old friends glanced at each other and, when it was clear Keane was not about to speak up, Fingal took it upon himself to play resident Seanchaí. The large man leaned far back in his chair; well away from his empty glass.

"Winston Eoghan Dwiggins."

"You're pulling my leg." The youngest member of the group accused.

"Wish I were. Winston was such a damn pain in the arse no one could be within two feet of him for more than five seconds—and that was the university record. He was a tea-totaler like and heaven help you if you were on the but end of one of his morality lectures. Anyroad, it was—what was it, Brendan? 1921? No, I lie. It was 1919—We were at university and Old Willow Winston had come to a holiday party with all his blustering and talk of eternal damnation. Well, your uncle and I, along with all the other students, got tired of this damn quick, so, when he went to get some punch we swapped it for some straight whiskey. Bloody eejit didn't know what hit him 'til the next morning when he had—as Dubliner's put it—the horrors." Michael was laughing so violently by the end of the story his entire body shook in the wooden chair.

"He always did have a weak stomach, Old Winston." Keane added; releasing a large cloud of white smoke. Fingal's blue smoke mingled easily with the white until it all faded away into a dim haze.

"Sure, isn't that the truth." Fingal sighed. "Did you know the old boy's married now? Aye, three chillin's and a grandchild on the way. Makes you feel age creeping through your bones, don't it? Well, look at us; babbling on like a group of bloody women. I'm off now, but feel free to come for dinner tomorrow. My Madeline's cooking, and she doesn't try to serve that damn rabbit food." Any association between the small, furry animal and the good doctor was enough to make a man smile, and smile Keane did.

CHAPTER SIXTEEN

The victim's blood spilled over my hands in a thick, sticky stream of stench. The deathly odor brutally attacked my nostrils a split instant before the heavy corpse collapsed on my limbs with a deafening crash. An astonishing pain shot through my right leg as I wrenched the dead weight back into a sitting position and myself as far away from its steely stare as possible.

"Jesus, Mary, and Joseph!" I twisted myself around to face a pink-faced Mrs. McCarthy blocking the shed's small, wooden doorway with her well-filled frame. I took the flush on her rounded face as an effect from winter's cold and not my seemingly uncanny knack for being tread underfoot. "And me just getting a hand on the laundry. Don't be mumbling those apologies now, bye. I hear 'em enough to know you're always sorry. But sure, isn't it the professor who says it'll be that monster that kills you and not my rolling pin." I guffawed audibly; sending a cloud of breath like a burst of white cigarette smoke.

"A motorcycle—my motorcycle is hardly a monstrosity. I keep it in excellent condition."

"Could have fooled me, so you could. All that metal and noise; screeching about like a cat who got it's tail slammed in the door and—Saints preserve us—all that grease. I'll start heating the water for a proper bath. No doubt it'll take a week just to get the ring off the tub when you're done. Mind you don't touch anything on your way up. Lord knows all I need is an arm and a leg of grey prints on the walls."

"'*Out, damn spot*!'" If Mrs. McCarthy wagged her head and pursed her lips.

"And you're no Lady Macbeth, to be sure. Now, off with you til wash."

In my life I found battling Hitler and his alliances far less daunting than disobeying Keane's long suffering housekeeper. She stepped well aside as I passed only to rush ahead to open the doors and guard her precious walls. (Heaven help the poor soul who brushed against her walls.) If she was this careful about Keane's house, I always dreaded how neurotic she must be about her own.

It took a great deal of soap, but the grease and grime at last dissipated into the sudsy waters, along with the slight drops of blood from my scraped ankle. The phonograph in the other room blared out some only partially intelligible song, of which I was able only to piece together the final line.

What good would it do . . .

What good indeed. It was a rare occurrence for me to be so completely enthralled with such a tale of sickening romanticism, but the vocalist leapt so skillfully—so casually—from word to word like few others ever could. It was as if the song meant so much to his own heart and soul you could not help but be dragged along in its wake. I had no doubt the young singer would quickly become a name that echoed throughout the ages of time: a legend.

Suddenly a crisp rattling, like the tinkle of china, sifted in around the band's scratchy music. The telephone, I thought begrudgingly. With any luck it would be one of Mrs. McCarthy's loose tongued friends, rather than a worried mother begging for an appointment with Keane. It seemed like every week there was another one mourning over the fact her boy wasn't "living up to his potential" or "lagging about" instead of doing his schoolwork. The first time I witnessed one of these desperate parents, I could have sworn Keane would have hurled the mother out bodily into the rose bushes after clapping the child about the ears. He did neither of these things, nor any variation of such. It most every case, save the few legitimate worries, Keane was able to diagnose various degrees of puer adolescentia, prescribe a full hour's play outdoors for the youth, and sent them both away: the mother feeling relieved in her duty, and the child with a fist of humbugs from the jar on Keane's desk.

You may not have heard of puer adolescentia before, but allow me to assure you it is a legitimate, infectious disease easily spread between those ages three to eighteen (and sometimes later in life, depending on the severity). There really is no immediate or faultless cure, as Keane has attested many times to sobbing women and angry fathers, but pray take into account everyone has, at some point, survived this fast spreading illness.

Puer adolescentia: or translated, Child's Youth.

My amusing reminisces were ripped from my grasp as a fist banged ruthlessly at the lavatory door. I leapt from the now cool waters, erotically dried my chilled, damp skin, and had managed to tie the rope of my dressing gown before flinging open the door.

"Mrs. McCarthy, hadn't you heard? The bloody war's over." The housekeeper eyed my wet, unruly appearance with all the grace I had come to expect.

"It's not that at all. That was the professor on the telephone. Asked if you could go back there." The hairs on the back of my neck shot up. Keane was, at best, temperamental and a bit demanding every now and again, but he wasn't the sort of man to ask me to do anything like this. No, he would wait for me to show up at the door and feign surprise I hadn't done so sooner. But things change, didn't they? Acceptations could be made. But if that were so, why was Mrs. McCarthy's face so pale; near transparent. No, Keane was not suddenly falling prey to sentimentality.

There had been an accident.

PART FOUR

Being Irish, he had an abiding sense of tragedy,
which sustained him through temporary periods of joy.
-William Butler Yeats

CHAPTER SEVENTEEN

Fools most always come in a set of three. (There were the Three Stooges, after all.) But now, as I flew bodily into the Keane family house out of the wretched cold, it struck me I had broken that tradition. I had become the forth fool.

I stomped snow from my boots, while at the same time crushing the sacred art of comedy. Michael, Thomas, and Keane all sat comfortably in the sitting room. (All breathing, might I add.) I could hear Catherine bustling about the kitchen, so she had not been the source of trouble that brought me so speedily back to the blue painted house. When we first arrived Keane said no person with a drop of Irish blood would return willingly to their homeland. While that may be so, he obviously believed me in need of a little persuasion. Despite my frozen, blue-tinted skin, my blood boiled and it was all I could do to wring the edge of my leather coat and not Keane's blasted neck.

"Lawrence," Keane greeted with an easy smile. "You made excellent time. I take it you had a good trip?" I peeled off my soaked gloves and threw them in his lap.

"Like bloody hell I did. Do you know what I went through just to get here as fast as I did? I'll be lucky if I don't come down with half the diseases in Europe after this. Damn it, Keane, I—" My rant was interrupted by a chuckling from beside the window; deep, overpowering guffaws of masculinity. How did I not see him at the moment I entered? He was tall, perhaps a half inch taller than Keane, but, very much unlike my companion's slim, guard-like frame, his was large with age-softened muscles. He was a stranger, yet I had seen him before. Of course! There was a picture of the two of them in the study; or at least a younger, colorless, silent version. The man illuminated in the sun's fractured light was certainly more boisterous than his picture.

"By God, Brendan, you said she had a tongue on her and you were bloody well right." Keane chuckled gently from his perch in the armchair.

"Lawrence, may I introduce Doctor Fingal O'Malley. He's an old friend of mine from back in university."

"Older than that if you count the war." O'Malley added. "But that only makes us sound like a pair of old farts. Good to meet you, Miss Lawrence." Any panic I felt over the doctor's presence dissipated as he rambled over and shook my hand heartily and, by some miracle, my fingers were not crushed by his large palm. As Doctor O'Malley stepped away, I glanced at Michael. The bruising around his eye had nearly disappeared, save a slight yellow tint. I shivered slightly as a stream of melting ice ran down my neck. How convenient it was at that exact moment when Catherine bustled into the room.

"Joanna, what are ya doing lollygagging about in the cold? Sure, and you must be hungry from your journey. I'm fixing nice roast duck and dumplings, and they should be done in fifteen minutes or so. Plenty of time for you to change into some dry clothes and get warm. My, the snow is really reeling down, so it is. Of with you, so." As I was shoed up the wooden staircase, I was quickly reminded of a famous line from the Dutch philosopher Desiderius Erasmus. Women, can't live with them, can't live without them. And God had made me one of them.

It was exactly twelve minutes before I again entered the sitting room, and in that time nothing had faltered from its place. Thomas and Doctor O'Malley both smoked their pipes, while Michael and Keane remained partial to their cigarettes. As it was an unspoken law never to open the windows in winter (especially when it is snowing cats, dogs, and about a dozen other mammals asides) I very nearly got lost on my way to the wooden stool in the far corner of the room.

"Ye gods, it's bloody London in here." I exclaimed as I waded through the thick fog. "Any casualties?" A smile flickered across Keane's lips as he lit another cigarette.

"Ain't nobody here but us chickens." Michael replied in an albeit higher, sing-song tone. It had only been a few months since that song had been released in America, and already it seemed to have captured his heart.

"Speaking of poultry," Catherine began, armed in a floral apron. "Those poor ducks'l be stone cold if you lot don't hurry." Michael and Thomas made a beeline for the kitchen; dodging around Catherine in the process like two small children after sweets. "I set an extra plate, Fingal. No need for you to leave hungry."

"Catherine, you are an angel and saint in one." Doctor O'Malley said as he began walking toward the doorframe. I glanced at Keane, who still remained seated in the armchair, and apparently held no aspirations from rising from the position.

"If there isn't room enough in the kitchen, Lawrence and I would be fine eating out here." Catherine nodded solemnly and began filling two plates, one of which she set on the side table near me before walking a few extra steps to hand Keane the other. Even after she disappeared to join the others, we ate in silence. The duck turned tasteless in my mouth as I ate almost mechanically. Keane worked a bit slower; pushing the food around a bit before at last shoveling it into his mouth. It was done with dignity. Dignity. Everything with dignity. The conversation remained civil, at best, and silent at worst. Nary a word was said that was not thoroughly thought out for at least a full five minutes before. It was all planned; so perfectly organized as though it was being shot on film.

But two chairs remained empty in the kitchen.

The fire was naught but ash and the clock announced the midnight hour, but I was far from sleep's door. As appeared Keane. I had sat quietly—wordlessly—for the past several hours as he turned page after page of the novel that had been lying next to him when I entered. His silver glasses sat prestigiously on the bridge of his nose; his lips a thin line as his eyes followed the inked letters. This did not concern me. This was quite an ordinary, if not dull, observation. The hour was the variable. On most every occasion he would have long since gone to bed by this time—or at least insist I did so. But he did not. He sat and read. And read. And read, until I caught the briefest lull of his head as it nodded down toward his chest.

"It's late." I whispered, causing his head to jerk upward and his glasses to jar back into place. His voice was hoarse and dry against the wind's whispers.

"Go to bed then."

"Keane, I am not saying it for my own benefit. You nearly fell asleep in that chair."

"I did not. I merely leaned down to turn the page." Stubborn fool.

"You did and I saw you, so denying it will do nothing. Besides, a night in that chair would play havoc with a person's back."

"Lawrence, if you are tired go sleep, otherwise—" I jumped to my feet, threw off the afghan that had been so carefully tucked over his lap, and emitted a sharp gasp and the woolen covering fell from my hands. Keane sat in a pair of grey, tweed trousers. Or, more accurately, what was left of them. The fabric of the left leg had been cut away from midway up his thigh; exposing a pale leg made white by a thick bandage winding upward from his stockingless foot before stopping abruptly just below the knee. Sticking plasters and bruises dotted the portion above that, and, for the most part, his right leg appeared untouched. A stripe of dried blood stained his shirt at the arm, but I saw no bandages sticking out from his sleeve. A mercy anyhow. I fell back hard in my chair.

"My God," I breathed. "My God, what happened? How bad is it?" My curiosity was shoved brutally aside by a wave of his hand as those two, ice-blue eyes caught mine.

"Mere scratches is all. A twisted back or fractured rib at worst. But you are quite right, Lawrence, it is late and I am quite exhausted. However, I may need some assistance getting up those damn stairs." I noticed he was careful not to add the struggle it would be for him to so much as rise from the chair. If curiosity killed the cat then dignity killed the dog. I stood again, held my hands out to him palms up, and watched helplessly as pulled himself to his feet with a grunt. He always seemed so much taller when we stood side by side, but on that day it became a decided advantage as his arm slipped easily over my shoulders. My hand instinctively went to his back, but a sharp hiss through clenched teeth sent it scurrying down around his waist. It was an awkward position. To that there was no doubt for either party. Even so, my inevitable concern was ill fated to mix with the nervousness of our close proximity. Keane grunted.

"Lawrence, stop looking like a bull trapped in a blasted china stop. I am not about to collapse or shatter on the floor."

"Are you sure?" I felt his hand squeeze my shoulder, and I needn't look up at him to know he was smiling gently.

"Quite. Now, if we could just—" He nodded toward the hallway and began taking a few experimental steps; tentatively measuring his movements to half his normal gait. His military posture was magnified by a selection of painful injuries and perfectly mimicked those injured soldiers limping back to battle. I shook my head violently. Many of them did not return—could not return. How many bodies had Hitler and his Nazis thrown into long, unmarked trenches; their naked limbs jumbled together with the hundreds of thousands of others. Cold, rotting flesh hidden beneath a soil of lies and limp with those last few moments of utter, debilitating hopelessness. When they were alive they had been pale skeletons, but now, black flesh separating from fragile bone the world had been ripped open in sickening transparency.

Keane stumbled slightly and the weight on my shoulders grew heavy enough for me to stop and allow him to regain his footing. It had been nearly a week since last I saw him, and I knew not whether it was my eyes or the light that tricked me. His suit seemed to have been tailored for a man half a stone heavier and the natural paleness of his features had whitened further. His electric blue eyes, while still sharp, had sunken ever so slightly into rings of darker flesh. But this did not matter in the slightest as he staggered and I was again faced with the brunt of his weight. No, these did not matter. He was alive.

When we finally reached the staircase I switched sides that he could balance himself between the railing and my shoulder. It was a slow but efficient process; completed by an occasional "Bloody hell" on his part. His limp had lessened everything considerably the further we journeyed through the sitting room, but the stairs were another necessary evil that challenged his footing and waning strength. At last we reached the guest room and Keane carefully lowered himself onto the edge of his bed. I helped him maneuver his arms out of the tweed jacket; a task considerably more difficult than it ought to have been. Too much motion in his shoulders caused his jaw to clench, while keeping the battered muscles still created a stiffness that induced a serious bout of cursing. When the damn jacket was hanging over the bedpost, I made a unanimous decision to solve—or at least alleviate—the situation through one of the techniques that remained infallible to the Irish and favored by the British. I traveled back down the stairs after a large glass and a bottle of Jameson whiskey.

Keane had made some progress in my absence, but admittedly very little. His sinfully unsymmetrical trousers remained, though the charcoal-grey suspenders had been abandoned on the floor. His tie hung limply over the bedpost beside the jacket—damn jacket—I myself had placed there. The objects screamed disorganization, though perhaps more as some form of abstract art, rather than a tornado's lifeless trail.

Keane himself was an entirely different matter altogether.

He still sat painfully erect on the edge of the mattress with a cigarette pinched artfully between his long fingers. Were I to mention these points alone one would have remained completely oblivious to the amusing—and still rather concerning—aspects of the situation. Clothed in the last remaining articles of his tweed suit, his shirt hung open; exposing thick bandages binding the lower portion of his pale chest. (Or, more specifically, I thought, the ribs.) A thin, almost feminine gold chain hung around his neck with a small, coin-like metal dangling from the middle.

I waited patiently for Keane to stab the final puffs of his cigarette into the empty ashtray on his nightstand before handing him the glass and adding a generous dose of the dark liquid.

"There, that should help a bit." I said, shoving the cork back into the neck of the bottle. Keane swirled the whiskey around in his glass, smiled, and began to recite in his warm, crisp english—

"'*Have more than thou showest,*
Speak less than thou knowest,
Lend less than thou owest,
Ride more than thou goest,
Learn more than thou trowest,
Set less than thou throwest—'"

"—I swear, Keane, even think about finishing that quotation and, injury or not, I will slap you." My companion chuckled and downed every last drop I had poured before holding it out for another round. I obliged. "Mind you don't get drunk on the stuff."

"Lawrence, it would take a great deal more than this watery swill to down so mighty a warrior . . . all the same," He took a long, slow sip of the strong liquor. "I shall heed your advice."

"Thank you." I resisted the urge to tap his shoulder and moved off toward my bed. It was a much safer thing to stare at an ordinary wall than those blue eyes of his. No amount of grease paint, no matter how eloquent the facade, he saw right through it without so much as a blink. I lay quietly as the light click of a bottle was drowned out by the burbling of poured drink.

To a gentleman and a scholar... and if the truth be known, sir, a great judge of Irish Whiskey.

I smiled deftly to myself, for Keane was easily all these things and a great deal more. He was an Irishman; born into the land of scholars and saints, and yet insisted he was no saint himself. And yet he performed miracles enough to cause doubt in my mind. I was as he was, a born and raised Catholic, but any Catholic who claims to be a good Catholic is really no Catholic at all. But, though Jesus and all his works should be rightly praised, there was one Keane did and the savior did not.

Jesus never threw a man into a rosebush.

I rolled over onto my back and stared at the ceiling for a short while before whispering into night's dismal haze.

"Keane, I—"

"—Not now, Lawrence. Tomorrow. Wait until tomorrow. I will tell you everything then. Yes, I do mean everything. But tomorrow, not tonight." My companion leaned cautiously back onto the mattress before pulling the bedclothes up over his bandaged chest. His breathing, though a bit labored, steadied into a constant rhythm. Then his voice came again, quieter this time but with the same clarity and gentleness I had grown so accustomed and—yes, I will admit it—terribly fond of. Even so, it took a moment for my mind to realize he was not speaking to me directly, but rather reciting with an ever flowing eloquence.

"'*Be not afeard: the isle is full of noises,*
Sounds and sweet airs, that give delight, and hurt not.
Sometimes a thousand twangling instruments

*Will hum about mine ears; and sometime voices,
That, if I then had wak'd after long sleep,
Will make me sleep again: and then, in dreaming,
The clouds methought would open and show riches
Ready to drop upon me; that, when I wak'd
I cried to dream again . . ."'*

CHAPTER EIGHTEEN

"Three days!" I shouted. "You were hit by a car—nearly killed—and didn't bother telling me for three days!" Keane shifted uncomfortably in the armchair. He had forgone the struggle of his jacket and instead sat stiffly in his shirtsleeves with the buttons undone to his naval.

"Really, Lawrence, it isn't so bad as that." Keane's steady words were contradicted by a slight flinch as Doctor O'Malley pressed the cold end of his stethoscope to his pale, bandaged chest.

"It isn't? By God, Keane, what if—what if you had died and I wasn't here? What would Mrs. McCarthy do then?" What would I do?

"Be reasonable—"

"—Reasonable." I scoffed. My voice was harsh and rough in my throat "Forgive me, I forgot I am dealing with reasonable gentlemen. It was very reasonable of that madman to run you down. Should I thank him? That sounds like the reasonable thing to do." My companion gazed up at me with a sudden gentleness as the doctor stepped away.

"Well, Fingal?" He asked, doing up his shirt buttons. Doctor O'Malley shook his head with a long breath.

"You are a very lucky man, Brendan. A very lucky man. From what I can tell without another x-ray—and let's not go through that argument again—the worst of it seems to be a few fractured ribs. Your leg and back should heal fine if you try to exercise mildly and mind they don't get infected. Speaking of which, are those bandages alright? Good. I'll come by later this evening to change them. No, don't get up. Miss Lawrence can see me out." I silently led the doctor into the hall, retrieved his cap and coat, and watched him bramble out into the cold. His large frame could not disappear into the bustling river of people, but it did fade away into the current. Keane was standing, though rather uncomfortably, against the fireplace's wooden mantle when I returned: a fresh cigarette poised in his hands.

"Keane, we need to talk."

"The temperature doesn't seem quite so bad today. Would you mind if we walked then? Rest can be a wonderful thing, but too much of it can turn a man's legs into stiff boards." As if to accentuate his words, he gingerly flexed his injured leg and winced.

"Someone tried to kill you by running you down with an automobile, and you want to walk? In broad daylight?"

"Don't be so tiresome, Lawrence. You know where to find my hat and coat."

I SINCERELY BELIEVE, in my twenty-four years of experience, that it is impossible to be truly angry with Keane for a long period of time. Especially when you have secrets enough of your own to balance the scale. The temperature had indeed lessened its bitter hold somewhat, though neither one of us believed it would last much longer than a few hours at most. The walk did seem to do my companion some good; his limp lessened considerably and, as we passed the butchers, I noticed him slipping my arm through his.

"The city has changed since last I was here." He began, glancing down toward me. "But I suppose that's the consequence of leaving only to live elsewhere."

"Even if you had stayed it would have happened. You can't stop change, just as you can't help the world from spinning on its axis." Keane sighed. A thick cloud of white appeared in the cool air.

"You're right, of course." We continued walking down the streets I had come to know then quickly turned down a road to which I was unfamiliar. It was a road like any other road; buildings and factories side by side as they lined the busy streets. Suddenly he stopped and nodded toward a medium sized establishment further down the way. "See that? My father started that steel business back in 1887. It was his proudest accomplishment. Thomas owns it now, and does a fine job of it, I imagine."

"You know, Keane, I don't think you've ever really spoken of your father before." Keane glanced at me before immediately turning his attention back to the grey building.

"No, I haven't, have I? To tell you the truth, Lawrence, I can't remember all that much about him myself." A dimness came to his eyes. The lines on his face had meaning now; the ones of laughter far newer than the crevices that furrowed his brow.

I felt his hand brush mine for an instant, though it was shielded by leather gloves. A brush was all it was, but that seemed enough for him to clear his throat, turn around, and begin a slow, measured walk in the opposite direction.

"Well, Lawrence, did you manage to accomplish much on your holiday before I dragged you back?"

"You didn't drag me back, though you were not entirely honest about the pretenses." The briefest smile played at the edge of Keane's lips.

"And for that I do apologize. But let's discuss your writing. I take it sales are still up?"

"Let's put it this way: you, sir, are in the presence of a very successful young woman." I stuck my nose up in the air, and at last Keane did laugh. A full, deep, hearty guffaw that always reminded me of a militant sea captain. His arm tightened on mine as he leaned bent his head down near my ear.

"I have no doubt in that, my dear Lawrence. No doubt whatsoever." He straightened himself again with a hand to his lower chest. "Now, I believe in the old saying '*a man's food should stick to his ribs*', and Lord knows my ribs are in need of being stuck back together."

THE DUCK WAS PACKED; cramming Keane and I shoulder to shoulder against the wall. Every so often my companion would interrupt his eating with a sharp flinch as some passerby inadvertently hit his injured leg. He seemed a great deal better than last night, but he drank fiercely; putting back long draws of stout in between bites of potato. I picked the slice of bread from my plate and began to slather it in butter.

"I was unaware the sale of my novels would put you in such an excellent mood. Or could it be you have found some new lead in my absence?" Keane cut through a piece of—what can only be described as pork—and skewered it with his fork.

"Lawrence, I am convinced you know me far too well. Yes, I have found some new evidence, but we can discuss that later. Right now—" My companion was slowly cut off as the burbles of conversation melted into a tremendous roar. Four relatively young man in uniform edged their way through and plucked the obese, bearded man from the crowd. It was the same one Keane had drank with until I had to drag him from the pub. The same, though now it was this man who was being shackled in handcuffs and slowly led back toward the door. In an instant Keane's hands were on the table as he pushed himself onto his feet and raised his voice with the countless blither.

"Sergeant Walsh?" The scrawny man glanced around a moment before breaking off from the other guards to come to our table. An overconfident grim played across his already ridiculous face as he zealously pumped my companion's hand.

"So it's yourself, Professor. Good to see you up and about after that fall you had. Can't say it doesn't happen around here from time to time, but I must say I was surprised to find it happening to you." Keane nodded his head politely, but those familiar eyes had a grey glint of steel. His voice; however, remained perfectly even and civil.

"Sergeant, may I introduce you to my friend, Miss Joanna Lawrence." The guard touched his head before immediately turning back to Keane with a disgustingly self-satisfied glow.

"So, Professor, I caught my man."

"Indeed, you caught *a* man, Sergeant. May I ask what evidence brought you to this individual?"

"Sure, it was easy, so. Funny you didn't think of it yourself, sir, but I suppose all that learning jumbles your brains a bit." It sounded like the eejit was speaking from experience. My sympathy poured out for the good many competent guards. "Sure, I just asked around a bit—got the word out, like—and sure enough Mr. Kinkade said it was his, so." Keane shifted his weight off his bandaged leg.

"You mean he admitted to both murders?"

"Like a murderer would tell. No, he just kept on deny'n the whole thing, but you can't expect a donkey to obey without a few good kicks in the shin." My companion winced, yet said nothing as the young man—if he could be called a man—marched away. Keane carefully sat again, but leaned away from his meal and pulled out his cigarette case with a near military precision.

"We had boys like that during the first war: ambitious, obnoxious, and, in the end, most of them dead. Not even they deserved such a fate." His voice was soft, almost wistful, as though he was reminiscing of a dream before fading back to sleep.

"War has a tendency of showing the enormous divisions between the good and evil in every man."

"And, as though one world crisis was not enough, we had another. I know men—good men—who fought and clawed their way through the first, only to watch their sons die in the second." Keane sighed heavily, a thick cloud of white smoke entering the atmosphere. "Is it right, Lawrence? Is it right that, in certain terms, I have lost nothing in this madness? I had tucked myself away behind my books and my theories while boys were slaughtered by the thousands. Infants—scarcely born into this world—were removed from it for Hitler's target practice. By God, I should have done something."

"You could do nothing."

"I could have enlisted."

"And returned just as broken and traumatized as they were?" If he returned at all.

"A great many Irishmen—"

"—Stop it. Haven't you considered that the neutrality of Ireland is perhaps the only thing that stood between you and the front lines? The only thing between you and an unmarked hole six feet under the dirt, if you were fortunate enough to be buried at all. You did all that you could, which was a great deal more than most. You can't blame yourself for what can't be helped." I glanced away for a moment, sucking in lungfuls of air stained with liquor and tobacco. "Just as you can't blame yourself for Bridget. Listen to me, Keane, it wasn't your fault. None of it."

"I could have stayed." He muttered. "If I hadn't gone to Dublin for that holiday, I could have protected her, convinced them she wasn't dangerous to anyone. She was only a child, Lawrence. A child. She was scarcely of the world before she was thrust into that Godforsaken place. I could have seen her more, written more . . . " Keane looked down to find his cigarette case empty and the glass at his arm equally dry. I reached into my jacket and brought out a package of Sweet Afton cigarettes (one of Keane's favorites) and slid them across the table before leaning forward on my forearms.

"You once told me that regret was made for those who had no time for the future. But you have time. You survived getting hit by a car, for heaven's sake.

'As to the legitimate: fine word,—legitimate!
Well, my legitimate, if this letter speed,

*And my invention thrive, Edmund the base
Shall to the legitimate. I grow; I prosper.'*

Yes, Keane, I read your copy King Lear. It was perhaps one of the few true accomplishments I had when I returned to England. I read the inscription as well, though I fear my knowledge of Gaelic is rather incomplete."

"'*Three things that are difficult to understand; the mind of a woman, the work of bees and the coming and going of the tide.*' The men of this world may say many things about my sister, but no one can deny she had a grand sense of humor."

"From what I learned from the asylum, I would bet good money she got that feature from you." Keane's eyebrows shot upwards on his high forehead and his mouth opened and closed rather like a fish that had just been hauled out of the water. "I found their telephone number the same day I found that book. Keane, they told me you used to visit her weekly and, when you had been drafted, you saw her on most every leave. The countless letters you wrote to one another could alone have kept the postal service in business. You taught her to read and write, Keane. To live." By this time my companion was looking deeply at the package of cigarettes, his sturdily cut facial features almost rigid as if it somehow injured his masculinity by me praising him aloud. He was always a sailor torn away from the sea. The weight of a dignified—entirely masculine—reputation was worth more than a thousand pounds of gold. He was easily all of these, with the addition of an ever-present temper. I had known him well for the better portion of a decade. He had become my confidant. My companion. My greatest friend. My only legitimate friend.

And I had no idea how he would react to my next words.

I cleared my throat—unnecessary though it was—and forced my hands to remain clasped tightly together.

"The asylum also informed me that a Miss Bridget Fiona Keane had been released and discharged to the private practice of a Doctor

McCladah about three and a half years ago. That's why she stopped returning your letters." At first I thought Keane was going to leap from his chair and run out into the streets, as if she would be there waiting for him without the decades of life between them. Instead, the seldom demonstrative man grasped my hand with a gentle fierceness and looked deeply into my eyes.

"Are you—Lawrence, are you sure?" I nodded. Keane let out a short sigh, as though he had been holding his breathe for the past few years just to hear someone say such a thing.

"Dear God," His voice trembled as his hands engulfed mine; his eyes far more blue than the purest ocean. "Dear God, I thought—Lord help me, I thought she was dead. But she's not. Thank God, she's not. Thank God." It is said that to be Irish means that you know, in the end, the world will break your heart, but, as Keane's face broke into that great smile, I found that the statement was only partially correct. To be Irish, truly Irish, means that the world will break your heart, but that day is not today, nor, God willing, will it be tomorrow. Nor the next day. Nor the day after. For beyond the sorrow comes a light; as bright as the sun and as pure as rain. And it will last as long as we let it and God permits it. This is the truth of every Irishman; live for today with those you hold most dear. Live for this moment. This second. This breath. Now.

And as long as we do that, no matter where you come from or where you are going tomorrow, we will never walk alone. Then, when the world breaks our heart, it does not break or spirit and we shall march on until the fading sunset. But fear not, with every sunset, there is a dawn.

CHAPTER NINETEEN

I had no fear. Or so I continuously repeated to myself as I followed Keane down the barred, cold, concrete halls. It was not that I had never been inside a gaol before, but, of all my fears, being crammed into a small cell with nary a true window was perhaps the most daunting. Tight walls of packed, grey stone brushed against my shoulders and sent cold trickles of air down my neck. The guard stopped, took from his belt a well polished key ring, shuffled through them, and shoved a chosen one into the hole with a violent twist. A loud, eerie screech echoed around my ears as he pushed the door open. Keane, tall though he indeed was, seemed to grow all the more so against the short frame of rock the door had sealed. The guard shifted away from the gaping hole, but remained close enough to block the exit were the need to arise. How comforting.

"Ten minutes and not a second more. I'll just be wait'n out here if Mister Bailly gives you any trouble." My companion glanced at me.

"Lawrence, you can wait out here if you'd rather." I shook my head. How considerate it was of him to not say "if you're afraid". If he had I would have seen it as a challenge and he could drag me in without protest. My feet followed him willingly through the tiny door into a room that seemed scarcely larger. Mr. Bailey was lying on a grey bench that ran along one side of the room, a thick, meaty arm slung over his eyes. His voice roared and echoed around my ears.

"If you didn't feck'n come here to bring me a proper jar, I don't want ye."

"Mr. Bailey?" The large man moved his arm from his face, glanced blearily up at my companion, and began the struggle of heaving his bulk up into a sitting position.

"It's yourself, sir. And the miss too. A damn sight better than those other feckers." I quelled the bright simmers of a smile. This man clearly had no reservations when it came to the more colorful language, even in the presence of women. How refreshing . . . and yet I still found him incredibly revolting. "They's been saying I killed those two buggers—God rest their souls—but I swear on my great-grandfather's buck tooth I—"

"—Quite right," Keane mercifully interrupted. "Quite right, and that is why we are here. Mr. Bailey—"

"—Sure, but doesn't everybody call me George. Like that feckin king those Yanks told to shove his taxes where the God damn things wouldn't see the li—"

"—George then. Would you mind telling us how your revolver came to be the murder weapon?" The large man folded his beefy arms across his thick chest.

"Sure, it wasn't mine anymore. I sold it."

"When?"

"Oh, a month or so back, so it was. Ya'know, a man could feck'n die of thirst in this here place. Feck'n drop dead from all the watery swill." Keane reached his hand deep into his overcoat pocket and produced a flask I had never seen before in my life. He tossed it casually to the man, who took a long swig. "You're a saint, sir. A feck'n saint. Now, as I was saying, I sold it to a shop on the corner. You know the one? It's a fine establishment, so it is, sells most anything it can carry. Used or new doesn't make one feck of a difference. I didn't have no need for the thing, so I didn't, and sold it to him for a nice little profit. 'Specially since it didn't work."

"You mean the firing pin?" The large man glanced at me.

"Sure, that's what it was. Never thought I'd live to see the day when a woman like yourself knew how to work a damn gun. This last war just about turned my mind to shite over all the changes. Women in airplanes, my God-damn ars—"

"—So you sold a gun that couldn't fire, no matter what you did?" Thank God for Keane, else I would likely be in a cell for intentional manslaughter.

"Sure, that's right. Didn't know why he bought it, but I wasn't about to argue with good money."

"'*To the eyes of a miser a guinea is more beautiful than the sun, and a bag worn with the use of money has more beautiful proportions than a vine filled with grapes.*'"

"William Blake." Keane added with the smallest, yet most rewarding, of smiles. *A man is a foreign book; unreadable unless you take the time to learn the language. And even then there are those words you will never fully understand.*

"A word, sir, if ye please?" The large man shifted forward on the bench, his eyes staring at the flask buried in his enormous hands. "Sure I know I'm no saint—couldn't even be called a gentleman—but I swear I didn't kill no one. Last time I held a gun toward another man was back in the wars, but them there was different, so they were. I was watching me ole comrades getting filled with lead and dropping just as hard. Sure, I'm not a good man, but I'm not a bad'un. Never even touched that revolver once I got back. Glad to get rid of it, I was. Too many boys died from the damn thing." The large man buried his face in his hands just as the cell door screamed of time's unstoppable path. *I have only seen grown men cry on select occasions, often as an observer to those long conversations between Keane and his patients, but on every occasion it was the same; you will never forget the sight and, as long as you live, it will haunt you.*

I TOOK KEANE'S ARM as we stepped back out into the realm of bees; a deep buzzing as hundreds of bodies shoved in every possible direction. Unlike humans; however, bees were admirable and worked together for a common cause. Here there were a thousand causes dripping with greed and personal gain. Two different worlds. Two separations without one understanding the other.

It took a great deal of time finding the shop, as it had been added long after Keane had left for England. Fortunately, his limp had lessened considerably and his back seemed to have shifted away from rigid pain by the time we entered the little establishment. The excruciatingly low ceiling was only marginally offset by the enormous cupboards and shelves lining the wall; practically creaking beneath the weight of miscellaneous merchandise. Men's hats sat unbrushed in toppling stacks. Ink stained writing paper was bound together with faded ribbons. Even a selection of pinstriped suits (horribly American in cut) hung on a piece of metal pipe crammed between two bookshelves. My attention merely floated over these things; however, until stopping at an open cigar box filled with pocket knives. For the most part, they were simple fold out blades, but near the bottom lay a multi-bladed pocket knife. The metal felt cool in my hand, yet wonderfully familiar. A deep chuckle echoed near my ear as Keane lifted the object into his fingers.

"We used to use those things in the navy. I still have mine somewhere, unless Mrs. McCarthy got rid of it."

"Mine was lost during one of the bombings when my bike slipped on a mud puddle. They are great tools, though."

"Can I help you find something?" The voice was without all the grease and ease an American might expect. In fact, the man's dark hair seemed entirely free from pomade but settled in straight, well combed lines. Much of the man's face was covered with a well kept beard, and his eyes were slow and absorbent, rather than flicking about like a cat's. Keane met the man's gaze and returned a smile.

"Yes, actually. Do you have any firearms? Revolvers?"

"Of course, sir." The young man leaned down behind the counter and pulled from it a large, flat drawer that had been carefully cushioned with tattered quilts. On top lay rows of guns, varying in both size and age alike. There were a few I recognized, though I suspected Keane knew more as he gingerly lifted one of the weapons from its restful state. The shopkeeper watched in awe as my companion balanced it easily in his fingers.

"Are ye looking for a certain kind of revolver, sir." Keane shifted slightly and laid the revolver back into the drawer.

"I used to own an Enfield number two. Do you have any of those, by chance?"

"'Fraid not. Sold one a few weeks back though." Keane's face fell, causing the lines on his forehead to deepen.

"I wish I had come earlier then."

"Wouldn't have done any good, if you don't mind my saying. The damn thing couldn't shoot even if you prayed to all the saints and angels in heaven."

"You mean you sold it, even though it wouldn't fire?"

"Aye, I was just as surprised as you are now, but the woman said it made no difference. Some decoration like for her husband's birthday."

"Do you know what she looked like?"

"Sure. Real thin. Long, dark hair. Little bit of makeup. Oh, and there was a boy with him. Fine looking lad, but real nervous. Cried too. Anything else, sir?"

"Yes." Keane grabbed a few boxes of cigarettes, as well as matches, and set them on the counter as I made my way toward the door. A group of children were playing across the street, nary a care in the world.

"How lucky they are." My companion commented, emerging from the shop mere seconds before he was handling a cigarette. I laughed. Some things never change.

"Stocking up, are we?"

"All men have their faults . . . " Keane's long hand dove into his coat pocket and brought out the multi-bladed pocket knife and pressed it into my palm. The moment my mouth opened; however, his palm stopped all words on my lips. "That shopkeeper only charged me three pence for the thing. It'll be a miracle if he's in business come spring."

KEANE'S FIST SWUNG toward my head; his face carved deep into cold marble. My body instinctively lunged backward, but not before his knuckles collided with my temple. I lost my balance and began to topple backward over the cliff's rigid edge where nothing lay between me and the fall's fatal surface. Just as my back began to arch in preparation for the tumble, my companion's long arm caught me at the waist and pulled me back onto the fallen log. He stepped off as I regained my balance.

"Then, once she had fallen into the water—still alive—the murderer strangled her near the shore before shoving her body back into the sea."

"Charming." I muttered, tugging at the collar of my jacket. In the past hour or so the temperature had plummeted further toward zero. "But if the woman felt she needed a gun, why knowingly buy one that wouldn't bloody shoot?" Keane sighed, crossed his arms across his chest, and leaned his weight onto his bandage-less leg.

"A facade most likely. Women—present company excluded of course—like to create that veil of illusion. She felt she needed a gun, but was afraid of killing; therefore, she bought one that wouldn't shoot."

"Hardly practical."

"Ah, but more moralistic to her. You see, Lawrence, in my profession I have found morals solely underlie much of our day to day life. They dictate what we can and cannot do. For instance, I knew a man once who honestly believed he would burn in Hell if he shot another man in battle. Upon the day his draft notice arrived, he burned his right hand until it was too disfigured to even hold a weapon. He believed in it so strongly he was willing to do whatever it took to avoid being put in a situation where his life depended on whether he would shoot or be shot."

"But Hitler—"

"—Yes, Adolf Hitler; the dictator who has given the world a prime example of corruption and hatred. Anyone who wasn't to his liking; dead. Do you know how many Jews, Catholics, Gypsies, and others were murdered in his camps? Somewhere over ten million. He was willing to kill all those innocent people—from the crying infant to the sick old woman—because he believed they were not pure or to his liking."

"Rather like the segregation in America." I bit my lip and kicked the snow against a nearby tree. "Keane, is it bad when one hates their own country?" My companion began walking up the hill, allowing me to follow just behind. His limp had almost disappeared, but I noted he was especially cautious through the fresh layer of snow. With each step I came to regret my questions. More so I was ashamed such a thing had escaped my mouth. What war can destroy patriotism can often bring together. The British were proud of their long and strenuous fight. The French were proud to be rid of Nazi influence. The Italians had been ridded of Mussolini. And Americans, well, Americans always seemed to be proud of everything they did. Perhaps it was simply because they were American; famed for their "melting pot" of a population and "liberty and justice for all". These were, of course, wonderful things. There were amendments and a three branched government and bicameral legislature. It was incredibly complicated, just as a body is complicated. Various limbs and organs perform specific jobs that the whole can function. But even then the eyes can be blind.

Keane reached the top and held his hand out to me for the last few steps. Rather than letting go when I was beside him, he drew me closer and once again threaded my arm securely through his.

"I don't think you hate the United States. You may not like it, but all nations have that barren ground lying far from morality and near corruption. However, I do understand what you are saying. Americans need a Mahatma Gandhi—a representative—to speak out against all the injustices commonplace in society."

"*You can shake the world.*" I quoted. Keane smiled.

"But remember the entire line, Lawrence: '*In a gentle way, you can shake the world*.'"

Mahatma Gandhi was shot the following year.

CHAPTER TWENTY

Michael strode into the Duck, ordered a pint, and sat down with the morning newspaper. He had already read it once, but between Joanna and Brendan's constant evaluation of society, he needed to read it again. A man needs to think for himself; to live without such commentary and banter. A man also needed the company of a woman from time to time, but bachelor life made it all the better. There wasn't a need to settle. He could travel if he liked; visit Athens or Pompeii without a thought to when he would return. It was a fine life, and it didn't take much imagination to see why his uncle had enjoyed it for so many years. It no doubt helped that Brendan Keane, professor of psychoanalysis (among a handful of other things), was not a bad looking man. In fact, in most circles, he would be considered quite debonair. Where his uncle had greying-blond hair, striking blue eyes, square-jowled cheeks, and a strong, slender build; however, Michael had inherited his looks from his father. He wasn't unattractive by any means, the women he met at university easily proved that, but his confidence had always been a balancing act. And a certain American had tipped the scales.

A bachelor is expected to pine for the brief company of beautiful women in clothing that seemed to have been made during a fabric famine. His tastes had always varied at this point, but never had he seen someone quite like her. She wasn't the conventional woman. Her hair wasn't long and she didn't wear skirts or high heels. She never wore makeup or, he thought, perfume. She didn't faint or scream, but bore the solid punch of a seasoned boxer. She was something new to him. So incredibly unusual he found himself drawn to her.

Up until the moment he tried to kiss her.

He had been slapped before, but it had always been playful, as though it was a right of passage before she kissed back. Michael had never minded those moments, as long as her nails didn't dig into his face. But never, never, had a woman—a girl—punched him. Worse yet, his uncle knew it.

A deep, slurred voice shook the wooden beam at Michael's shoulder. The enormous bearded man swung his arm outward violently, sloshing some stout onto the floor and scarcely missing the man behind him. Damn fool, Michael thought as he tipped his own glass back. But even fools can tell interesting stories.

"Sure, and that professor got me out, so he did. Easy as breath'n for him. Didn't take nothin more than a few hours too. That girl with him is a smart one, so she is. Not much of a looker, but could make some young lad a nice woman. If she knows how to cook, that is. Wouldn't want to marry otherwise, and still don't. The best way to a man is his stomach, they say, and, sure, whoever said that is a scholar. No doubt a good judge of Irish whiskey too—another one if you please. Sure, if she's as good a house woman as she is a smart one, some young lad's gonna have one hell of a future. Sure, and . . . " Michael finished the rest of his drink and pulled at his coat. Damn fool that man, he thought again as he slipped his arms through the sleeves. Any woman could catch a man through his stomach, but the woman got him through his eyes.

In one solid punch

CHAPTER TWENTY-ONE

"By God, Fingal, you're supposed to be a bloody doctor." Keane hissed as his friend, his old comrade at university, peeled away the bandages strapping his ribs. Uncomfortable was an understatement. My companion looked as though he was being tortured as strips of sodden white were peeled away to expose colored bruises and jagged, angry red lines. He sat near the fire on the stool, the flames sufficiently warming his exposed skin. Keane winced and turned his set jaw toward me. "And for heaven's sake, Lawrence, keep reading!" I glanced down at the stack of newspapers in my lap.

"On the twenty-eighth of November—"

"Louder, Lawrence. And be articulate. You never have any trouble being heard when it comes to your opinions."

"On the twenty-eighth of November, 1946, Miss Agatha P. Brown (twenty-three) was discovered dead in the alley near Gilbern's—"

"—A firearm shop—"

"—discovered dead in the alley near Gilbern's after several apparent blows to the head. Services will be held—"

"You can skip that part. Next?" I tossed the top paper onto the floor and glanced at the next heading.

"This one's from May of last year. A Miss Eileen O'Brian."

"Hold on, I think I knew her." Dr. O'Malley stated as he ripped a sticking plaster from Keane's back, causing a low string of heated curses. "Aye, I did. Nothing too out of the ordinary, though: wealthy, busybody, chairwoman on some smaller committees. Bloody bother if you ask me. She had a husband—John, I think—who died in England.

Only thing he left her was his money and gun collection. She moved here the same year, around 1935—or was it 1936. My memory isn't what it used to be." Keane shifted rigidly in his chair, a hand pressed on the bare, bruised skin at his ribs.

"Neither is your skill at removing bandages. Hurts like bloody hell."

"1935." I mused. "Keane, wasn't there some enormous robbery that year. Something about an airport and gold?"

"The Croydon Aerodrome robbery? Yes, that would be about the right time. Twenty-one thousand pounds worth of gold was stolen. There were three men suspected of the crime at the time, though two were later acquitted: Cecil Swanland, Silvio Mazzarda, and a mister—"

"—John O'Brien." I gasped. "Surely it's not the same one. The man must have been in his seventies when he was acquitted."

"Seventy-four. How old was Mrs. O'Brien, Fingal?" The doctor began unrolling a long strip of bandages.

"Oh, late sixties I'd say." Keane leaned forward in his chair.

"By God, Lawrence, we may be onto something. Here, hand me that newspaper." He scraped his eyes up and down the printed article until he suddenly stabbed his forefinger onto the inked sheet. "There! Look at this, 'Miss Eileen O'Brien was found dead in her house on the third of May. Cause of death strangulation with a gold necklace—' That's it!"

"What's it? Keane, we have read through at least a dozen papers now and I still don't see—"

"The guns, Lawrence, the guns. In every murder there has been one nearby—Gilbern's shop, Mr. O'Brien's collection, the one bought on the corner—but no one was ever shot."

"And all the recent, unsolved murders happened sometime after 1944." I added. Dr. O'Malley stood from taping the last strip on Keane's back.

"Doesn't sound like that cuts your list down much. A lot of our boys were coming back from war that year, as well as the year after.

Speaking of battles, Joanna, may I suggest you retreat to another room for a moment; because, Brendan, unless you want me to cut another pair of your trousers to patch up that leg, I'll need you to take them off." I smirked at Keane's shocked expression, brushed the papers from my lap, and quickly strode into the kitchen, where Michael and his mother were already sitting at the table.

"Oh, Joanna, would you like some tea?" Catherine began to push her chair back, but I shook my head.

"Don't bother, I'll get it myself. A refill, Michael?"

"Please." I filled the two cups and turned back to the woman of the house, who was reaching for her coat.

"Don't worry about me, dear. I'll just be popping off to the grocer's quick." As she bustled out the door I was again struck with the horror of how dull housewife work must be. Thank God I wouldn't have to do anything of the sort, and if any many even thought of such a thing—

I glanced at Michael's eye. It looked almost normal now, but it must have been quite a shot to warrant that little smudge of green at the edge. The color almost matched his eyes. So often has it been said eyes are the windows to the soul. As I looked at him; however, I was struck with just how green they really were. Surely that was how the grasses of Ireland looked in the summer when the world was actually warm and not snow covered. It seemed to be snowing more recently, but it still wasn't too bad. It was like a bruise, colorful and, at worst, a bloody inconvenience.

A light, polite cough interrupted my thoughts, and I realized belatedly I had been staring at Michael far longer than what is polite and just short of incredibly uncomfortable.

"Have a pew." He offered. I sat in the chair opposite him. It is always an awkward thing to be so close to someone who tried to kiss you. It was also a feeling I had no recollection of.

"So," I began, holding out the "o" until the sound was almost comical. "You've been to university?"

"Aye. I heard you have too. Good to hear it; the world needs more university women." It was a brave statement, and one I would have taken as a compliment toward femininity had I not questioned whether he appreciated more scholars in the world or more feminine company during his studies.

"I studied English literature."

"Mm. Shakespeare, Coleridge, and that?"

"Some, but I prefer Keats and Milton. Emile Durkheim is rather interesting when I can find a copy." Michael laughed; a dry, expressionless noise that seemed to echo emptily in my ears.

"Like my uncle." He stated plainly. For some odd reason I almost felt obligated to apologize; to try to set myself apart from Keane in his eyes, that I wouldn't feel so ashamed every time a similarity was found. Was that it? Was I ashamed? I didn't think so, but, in that long moment before the light returned to Michael's eyes, I almost believed it. But the light did return, along with a small smile. "Have you seen the library? No? You'd love it: books as far as the eye can see and further. I can take you, if that's alright, of course?" I drew in a sharp breath. Those green eyes were so clear against the dark shag of hair; so calm and collected one might have thought them an ocean of emeralds. His hand reached slowly forward on the table and brushed mine ever so gently before jerking away. When I did not move or lash out, they came again; laying carefully over mine that their warmth surged through my fingers. Finally I was able to nod slowly.

"I'd like that." Oh, how those eyes lit up at my words. How lightly his fingers grasped mine as his thumb ran slowly over my knuckles, causing a spark to surge up and down my spine. His voice had softened too. It was almost a whisper, yet I could have sworn a mountain would crumble at its command.

"Not tonight, though. It's almost dinner. Tomorrow then. Would two be alright?" I again felt my head bob up and down; this time somewhat faster than before and with a smile I would rather not admit to. "Tomorrow at four then." Michael smiled and gently squeezed my hand before he rose from the table and left without another word. I was somewhat gratified that he had not kissed my hand, for breathing had become suddenly difficult and each surge of oxygen seemed to burn my lungs. But it a good way, I thought. Never in my life had anyone treated me in such a way. It was as though I was being dragged around the earth at a dizzying speed and while my head screamed for me to stop, the rest of me allowed myself to be carried onward in the current.

THAT NIGHT SLEEP REFUSED to come for the longest time, and, when at last it did visit, it was not pleasant. I was thrown into a nightmare more vivid than most; color had become a weapon and sunlight a torch burning my flesh. It had been months since last the sandman cast so horrible a deed, but nightmares are not things one easily forgets. My limbs had been tied still with fear as I was thrown into a lake of sweat; my body writhing as it sunk lower through the pounding surf. A knife slashed through my flesh in long strokes, and with each lash came a picture more vivid than its predecessor. At first it was rooms; cold, dark, and so small the walls threatened to break my shoulders. Then the knife came again and I saw a young woman lying in a frozen alley atop a mattress of her own blood. It struck again and there was an old lady with blue-tinged lips and empty eyes. Then the woman came; skull smashed at the temple and her flesh bloated with water. Her son came next as mutilated slabs of flesh tossed together in sickening, unnatural positions. At last the knife stabbed downward, and I saw Keane. Two long, jagged cuts ran down the side of his face and his striking eyes had fogged over in an unfocused haze. His thin lips were almost as blue as his eyes. But the blood in which he lay motionless was warm and sticky in my hands. Suddenly the crimson began to spread and deepen until I was drowning in that as well. My throat constricted, and my lungs grew flat until deep inside me the last bits of life bubbled upwards in a final hopeless shriek that shook me into an hour that was neither night nor day. As my mind returned to stability, so did the sour taste of vomit in my throat and the stiff woodenness to my limbs and spine. It took longer still to realize the hands on my shoulders were not my own, nor was the buzzing a swarm of disorientated bees but a voice, deep and calm while retaining a bit of something that was completely unfamiliar to my ears. Fear, perhaps?

"Lawrence? For God's sake, Lawrence, wake up." I sat up and shook my head violently until the hands on my shoulders snapped upward to my face and held it at bay. "Lawrence, are you alright?"

"I'm not sick, if that's what you're asking." I sounded sick, though. Sick and tired of worrying about murderers and knives. Sick of growing up to see just how horrid the world really was. Perhaps I was sick.

I was only partially aware of the extra weight settling at my side so our shoulders touched. In my nightmarish haze I didn't notice the darkened rings at his eyes, nor wonder why they had never left. I was; however, well accustomed to the snap of the silver case, hiss of a match, and the scent of tobacco smoke spilling into the air. There was so much comfort to be found in these things, just as much as the brush of Keane's fingers as he tucked the quilt over my shoulders. It was not enough; however, as my body began to tremble with those images; scenes enough to make one's stomach turn to stone.

"Here." Keane carefully handed me his lit cigarette, and I took several long draws. Each puff made my shoulders relax and my head lean ever so slightly toward his. With a few good draws left in it, I handed the cigarette back to its owner, who thanked me with a low chuckle that made him shake ever so slightly.

"You could have your own, if you wished." He whispered quietly, but I shook my head.

"No, that would make me a smoker." At that Keane did laugh heartily, and I found myself incredibly disappointed when he stopped. For, without laughter, there is silence.

And a person doesn't have to be alive to be silent.

There was the brief smell of sulfur as another match took light, and, for a brief instant, I questioned what his ratio was between cigarettes and matches.

"Keane, you can go back to sleep. I'll be alright." My companion glanced down at me for a moment before staring back at a uniform spot on the wall.

"Had it occurred to you I might not find sleep my greatest friend either?" I was silent. Of course it had not occurred to me. Here we were, side by side, shoulder to shoulder, and yet my mind still felt so distant and completely detached from the rest of the world. My body screamed for sleep, but remained unwilling to succumb to its icy hands. It was a common enough problem. I had seen dozens of soldiers suffer from it, as well as a few people who suffered other traumatic events. I could even find it somewhere in my heart to forgive myself for this weakness.

But how strange it was to find Keane suffering from the same difficulty.

And yet he was. The dark shadows under his eyes were proof enough of that, not to mention the heavy sighs as white clouds fell into line; one after another until it was time to light another cigarette. It was a strange thing, but somehow comforting to know one is not alone in these matters.

That I was not alone.

CHAPTER TWENTY-TWO

I had no recollection of falling asleep, only the sluggish churning of the mind when one awakes. Gradually I pushed away the covers and sat up to face a window coated with fresh snow upon the sill. My skin tightened with cold's frigid grasp, yet somehow I remained warmed by the night's confessions. For so long in my life fear was a weakness, and one must never show weakness in times of war. It leaves a spot unguarded to the enemy's sword and often scathed by a sharp tongue or two in the process. When I found Keane in the kitchen that morning the dark shadows had not improved, nor had they worsened. They merely remained as a testament to his mortality.

His mortality.

Yes, I had been reminded of that far too many times on this trip. From his catching of a common cold or being hit by a car to this. This.

And I liked—dare I even say loved him for it.

I adored his mortality; because, it was perhaps the one thing that tied him to this earth as a man and not Heaven. He freely admitted he was not a saint, but no saint had ever been entirely perfect. Even Saint Joseph, the earthly father of the savior, was himself imperfect. Keane had a temper violent enough to rock earth and sky in as much his blood ran with a warm gentleness that might quell a giant's anger. He was as prideful as he was humble. Stubborn as he was generous. And, most of all, Keane was himself.

He pushed a cup of tea across the table to me as well as a plate of cold eggs. The rubber consistency of the latter meant nothing as my appetite was hardly existent, but I pecked away at them all the same.

There are some things in life one enjoys, but some one merely endures. Keane, on the other hand, sat behind an empty plate and was working on his second cup of tea. I looked up from my meagre breakfast to the window.

"Does it usually snow this much?"

"Hardly." Keane replied. "But what would the world be without a little snow every so often to make life interesting. The roads aren't bad though; so, how would you feel about going on a drive in the country?"

WHILE IT IS ENTIRELY true Keane hated motorcycles, he adored cars. He was also one of the best drivers I had the pleasure of knowing. I sat back in the passenger seat as he skillfully maneuvered along the roads at speeds that made me incredibly thankful it was too cold for cycling. His hands rested on the wheel in such a way his entire body seemed to relax into the leather seats. The automobile wasn't quite so nice as the one he owned in Devon, but it wasn't bad and, as well as it was handling the snow coated roads, I was not about to complain. It even had a radio, which Keane felt obligated to test; tapping his fingers in rhythm against the wheel and humming even the most intricate parts of Beethoven and Mozart. He looked so entirely at himself I found myself grinning, which quickly tumbled into laughter. Keane smiled and turned down the knob on the radio.

"I may have an ear for music," He chuckled. "But I am sure my humming would appall even a tone deaf dog." It was a lie, of course. Really he and I were both cursed with something near perfect pitch.

Keane suddenly made a hard left turn that shoved me into his shoulder.

"I take it there is a point to this madness."

"Madness?"

"Keane, you are a man driving with a purpose and would trample any unfortunate animal to get there." Another light chuckle echoed in my ears.

"Would it please some part of your femininity if I slowed down?"

"Not on your life." He made another hard turn. "Just be sure we arrive wherever we are going in one piece."

As it happened, the place Keane stopped was hardly more interesting than a stack of well-placed stones. The outside had been kept neat, but there was absolutely nothing extraordinary about it. The shudders had been painted brown, as well as the door and most any other thing that could be painted. The house was neither big nor small. Neither tall nor short. Neither long nor square. It merely existed, and that seemed enough to satisfy it.

Keane stretched his long body out of the car and I was struck, not for the first time, that he seemed better suited for big American cars, rather than the small ones Europe seemed so intent to produce.

"Come." He slipped a hand on my elbow and led us up the dirt walkway. Rather, it was a dirt walkway dusted with snow and layered lightly with brief patches of ice. My boot skidded on the latter of these and, though I managed to catch myself, my dignity had faltered. Keane smiled but said nothing. Damn the man. It was worse than if he had made some remark. Now I was to wait for the tiger to pounce at any unsuspecting moment. How unfortunate it was that that leering tiger had such clear, watery-blue eyes and a humor far more enjoyable than most. It was in this sliver I found comfort . . .

. . . until that same tiger knocked on the door.

It was a woman that answered; individualized only by her ordinary, dull face with the standard uniform of a woman to match. Her nose was a bit too big, her arms a bit too large, and her waist round and overbearing in comparison to her small frame. With her dark, black hair she almost looked Italian.

Almost, but not quite.

The Irish brogue I had come to expect was scarcely recognizable as every syllable ran together in a horse, low growl.

"Can I be helping you lot?" Keane, ever the gentleman, swept his hat off his head in one swift motion.

"My name is Professor Brendan Keane, and we have come to ask about a Miss Agatha Brown?" So that's what we were here for, clever devil. The woman; however, did not find it nearly so amusing as I. She crossed her arms across her ample chest and gave a doubtful harumph.

"Miss Brown? She died—God bless her soul—few months back. Murdered, so she was. Hit on the head til she dropped senseless. Awful way to go, that, though I can't say I'm altogether sorry she's gone." Keane raised an eyebrow, but his mouth stayed securely shut. Mine, of course, did not.

"Did you have a quarrel?"

"Hm? Not so much as a housekeeper can with their employer. She was asking for trouble, so she was. All that money she was always talking about." The woman leaned forward slightly. "Though, if I'd be a betting woman—and thank the good Lord I'm not—I'd wager sixty-pounds that her money wasn't all clean."

"Clean?"

"How she earned it like. I've been told I'm a grand judge of character, so I have, and Miss Brown had a past. I'd wager she was one of them floozies like: take money any way she can get it, no matter what man it is give'n it to her. Dirt of the earth, I'd say, so I would." Keane flinched ever so slightly; a slip I was able to catch only through a near decade of close association. His voice was cold but strictly polite as he positioned his hat back on his head and strode evenly back to the car. Every inch of movement seemed to suddenly pain him; his back was too straight and that limp—damn the thing—decided to make another appearance. At the moment I climbed into the passenger seat, his foot slammed down upon the pedals and sent the little car jolting along the horrid roads.

It was as close to flying as one could possibly come without fully leaving the ground, and, by the rigid set of his jaw, I doubted Keane was about to let up any time soon. The snow-dusted country became a blur. The trees, drunken men bending their branches down to keep their balance. Motionless rocks turned to brief spots among the white. I survived this for a thousand years when I felt my body suddenly surge forward in one violent motion.

We had stopped.

Keane leapt out of the contraption and stalked out along the countryside for a good hundred yards before throwing his back against a tree and ripping a pack of cigarettes from his pocket. He smoked feverishly; shunning the burning ends into the snow before immediately lighting another. Thick, white clouds billowed from his lips and drifted away in the wind. So many things are lost in the wind; so much time dissipated in brief hesitations. I did not hesitate this time. I slowly trudged up to the tree, pressed my shoulders against the half frozen trunk, plucked a cigarette from the package, and began slowly taking long draws of the tobacco. Unlike Keane, I was always slow about these matters; gradually inhaling and exhaling in smooth, calming motions. When the fire grew too close to my fingertips, I flung the butt into the white piling at my feet, and that was that. Keane offered me another, but I shook my head; content to remain leaning against the tree in silence's magnificent majesty. A brigade of fresh snowflakes tumbled aimlessly from the sky. One of these, a thick one the size of my thumb nail, landed softly on Keane's sleeve as he pinched another cigarette between his fingers. What an incredible thing to consider no two snowflakes are alike. One is made without another in its likeness. The subject of such a thing is quite elementary, perhaps obtusely so, and yet I could not ignore it. I could not make myself oblivious to so wonderful a thing; so beautiful a creation I could catch in the palm of my hand. But, as all good things—truly good things—they never last. They disappear into a wetness that soon becomes a microscopic dot in one's mind. I leaned a little more into the tree; a little nearer to Keane. No, no two snowflakes are made alike, but each are pure as they fall from the sky. Each sparkling crystal remains clean until it finds its destiny is to be soiled and trodden on.

Such is life.

Oh, we may not be made for such a pessimistic purpose, but the story is all the same no matter how you look at it. There are times in our life when there is nothing but heavy boots pounding us further and further into the grime of work. So often one needs that other person to pull them upwards out of the dirt; upwards into the sky in which hope—a new hope—may be restored in full. And when you are able to stand side by side with that person in winter's cold with nothing but silence and a few cigarettes between you, well . . .

. . . that's something special.

Eventually Keane grew tired of the constant pattern between cigarettes and matches and flicked the final end into the air before tugging the edges of his coat collar. The snow had thickened, not horribly, but enough to encourage us to climb back into the car. Keane started the engine and slowly coaxed the machine into a gentle glide along the roads. Bits of snow fell from the brim of his hat onto his shoulder as he maneuvered gradually around a rather daunting turn and settled back further into his seat. I watched patiently as his thumbs rubbed along the steering wheel's edge with every turn and twist. It was not the same way we had come. No, this route was far longer. But I did not mind in the slightest. I was content watching the snow trickle down, the scenery sluggishly passing my window, and the steady profile of my companion. From this position I saw the end of the scar peeking out from beneath Keane's hair. Through the years—decades, I reminded myself—the brief stretch of puckered skin had flattened and remained only marginally discolored from the rest of his skin. How much I had learned in such a short time. I had seen Keane both as a boy and an old man, but, most of all, I had seen most every aspect of the man until my mind filled those gaps he had always left empty to me. The puzzle was not finished, nor, I thought, would it ever be. But I had gathered a few more pieces for the collection: a few more scars and bruises tucked away in the past.

Suddenly a throaty cough echoed through the small machine, followed by a series of sputters and completed by a low groan as the car eased to a pained stop. Keane fiddled with the keys a bit before slamming his hands against the wheel.

"Damnation!" He growled and flung himself back out into the surmounting cold. I joined him as he propped open the lid and pushed his hat back on his head; resting his hands on his hips as he surveyed the innermost workings of the car.

"Please tell me we're out of gas." I muttered as I stalked around to his side. He grunted and reached his hands into the collection of wires.

"Hardly. It's the engine. We may be able to—" Keane leapt back as two wires sent a series of sparks flying at his face. I stepped forward and began to survey the grease-coated organs. Of course, he was right. It was the engine. Keane shut the bonnet and climbed back into the driver's seat. I didn't need to glance at my watch to know it was close on noon.

"Catherine packed a lunch for us, I think, and there are some rugs if it gets too much colder, and—Lawrence?" Keane padded down his pockets. "Lawrence, is there any chance you have another pack of cigarettes?"

CHAPTER TWENTY-THREE

It was nearly four when Keane and I at last staggered into his childhood home; thick layers of snow caking our boots and pants. Keane shed his coat at the door, then his jacket on the couch, before at last settling himself in the armchair near the fire. No doubt the finest example of a man of habit. I followed in his lead and pulled the wooden stool so close to the fireplace my stocking feet would ignite if I wasn't careful. With a long grunt, Keane reached for the side table and neatly poured two small whiskies. He was half done with his when the door burst open again and another figure came barging in; a thick, heavy coat softening his figure and a hat tied to his head with a bright red scarf. When he saw me I wanted to topple into the fire, stocking feet and all, until I could flit away as freely as ash. I knew there was no hope.

"Joanna?" Blast. "Joanna, where were you? Are you alright? You scared me half to death. At first I thought you were just being ladylike—fashionably late and all that—but almost two hours—"

"—I'm sorry, Michael. Really, it was an accident. The engine wouldn't start and we were out in the country. I would have called, but the nearest house we walked to didn't have a telephone, and then . . . " It is really very undignified to make excuses for one's self. And it is worse to have to repeat in writing what is said in those brief moments of weakness. However, as I tried to shorten the story—which, of course, made it longer—Keane sat silently and finished his whiskey, then a second. Rather than pouring a third, he stood and held his palms upwards. And they say only God can make the earth quiet.

"Michael, dear boy, it really was my fault, not Lawrence's. She was helping me with a problem and, well, que sera sera." Whatever will be, will be.

"Really, Michael, I *am* sorry. We could go tomorrow if you like?" I watched the young man mull over the question for a long moment, close his eyes, sigh, and, at last, smile.

"On one condition."

"Name it."

"We go first thing in the morning so you can't forget, and," The smile stretched into a grin. "We will go for lunch afterwards."

"Deal." Thank God Michael was satisfied with shaking hands. I wouldn't know how to react to anything else. A grunt behind me created a marvelous distraction.

"Wonderful. Now, if you two have that straightened out, this old man would rather like to get warm before I turn into a bloody ice cube."

"Lawrence, how would you react if I asked you a personal question?" I rolled over in my bed and propped my head up on my elbows to face the man sitting on the other mattress.

"Oh, about the same as a normal question, I would think. Why?" Keane tugged at his tie until it hung loosely around his neck. Through the dark of early night; however, it looked rather like a snake skin. My companion peeled the snake from over his shoulders and flung it over the bedpost before starting on his shirt buttons. On most every occasion I would marvel at the skill with which he conducted such simple matters, but tonight it seemed to require his eyes watching the button slip out of the hole.

"If—if I were to ask what you thought of Michael—"

"—As a friend?" Keane's fingers slipped from his shirt buttons.

"Or something more serious."

"Keane, I don't think one can get much more serious than a devoted anthropologist. With the Druids and vikings and—"

"You haven't answered my question."

"I wasn't aware you had actually asked." He fumbled his way through the last button before finally looking up at me. I sat up until we were eye level. "Look, Keane, I don't know what I think of him. He's nice and all, but really I haven't thought of anything beyond that." Keane's chest heaved slightly as his back went rigid and his chin went up like a man about to face a firing squad.

"I see. Thank you as always, Lawrence, for you honesty. I understand your position. Sleep well." I lay back on my bed, turning my attention to the white gusts hurled at my window. For once in my life, I wasn't entirely certain Keane did understand. Damn the man, he knew me far too well.

And yet we were complete strangers.

CHAPTER TWENTY-FOUR

Keane was gone by dawn; gone, but not far from my mind. Then again, he never was. Michael arrived at ten and we set off for the library in his car. It wasn't new by any means, but it ran beautifully. The library was magnificent. There is no better word in all the world to describe such a piece of heaven. Rows and rows, floors and floors of books edged upwards toward the sky. Michael followed at my heels as I plotted about the shelves like a hound on the hunt. It was a world entirely of itself. Jules Verne had created nothing its like, nor Doyle, nor Dickens, nor any other being who had set foot upon the earth. It was a wonderland set above the droll hubbub of daily life. It was a miracle.

And it was at my fingertips.

Some time later, when Michael had gone off to do some research of his own, I brought an armload of treasures to a table and sat. Some I had read a thousand times, and others not at all. But it didn't matter. That was the glory of it all. It didn't matter how many times I had read the book, for here the words became fresh again and I could taste every syllable on my tongue. It was there, when time had no importance or draw on my life, that I found a most striking truth. Truths can often be found when one does not search for them, and so it happened. It reached from the page and struck me violently across the face as Sir Robert Chiltern raised his voice in defense.

-*No one should be entirely judged by their past.*

Indeed not, I scoffed to myself. But do we not? Do we not say you are you and I am I because of what happened on the day of our birth? Do we not separate ourselves from some ill perceived ideals? Lady Chiltern answered somberly.

-*One's past is what one is. It is the only way by which people should be judged.*

-*That is a hard saying, Gertrude!* Her husband replied quickly.

-*It is a true saying, Robert.*

And was it not? Was it not true that we are all guilty of some premeditated murder? Yes, murder! Not against another being's physical self. The world had placed laws securely against such an evil. But what about the people's souls? There were no laws against that; no safe haven against the prejudices you or I may have learned from our mothers, and our mother's mother, until there was a divide sinking into an abyss at our feet. When would the day come in which an Englishman and a German could shake hands—or even walk on the same side of the street—without consideration for the years of blood spilled between them? When would the day come when Catholics could look upon the world free from scorn and judgement? When would the day come when women were not housewives, or cooks, or maids, or any of those things without having some sister who had gone to university and bettered herself? And when would the day come when all Americans understood that the person—the ideal—was not colored or white, but colorblind?

Should I live to see such a day, I would die and be glad of it. But the odds were not in my favor. Keane was right, though he is rarely wrong. I never hated the United States. But so often we fear what we cannot understand. So often we hide between a wall of strong biases before we would step out into the truth without the delusion of protection.

I shook my head and turned the page. Here I again stopped as Lady Chiltern again took up her voice.

-*Compromise? Robert, why do you talk so differently tonight from the way I have always heard you talk? Why are you changed?* Sir Robert Chiltern shifted in his seat.

-I am not changed. But circumstances alter things.
-Circumstances should never alter principles!

"An Ideal Husband? Joanna, I'm surprised." Michael sat down across from me with an amused grin playing at his face. I sat up indignantly.

"And why not? Oscar Wilde was a genius."

"Yes, among other things." By now the young man was smirking. For, while Wilde had been one Ireland's most revered playwrights, it was not his art that so often sent hidden laughter among the lower classes.

Michael quickly cleared his throat and stood from his chair.

"Now, how about a late lunch?"

The restaurant was not large by any means, but the food was incredibly good, as well as the wine. I had never been accustomed to such things, but I felt out of place with my heavy wool sweater and RAF jacket. But no one paid a second thought to that reminder of the war.

War: a three letter word that forever changed the minds of both mice and men.

Michael proved an expert when it came to pouring even amounts of wine into our glasses while scarcely allowing his silverware to clatter on his plate. The conversation was not such a simple affair.

"You seem to do a lot of traveling with my uncle." He said; cutting into his steak with long, quick lashes.

"Some." God, uncle made Keane sound so dreadfully old when Michael said it. Keane wasn't old. He was only a little over fifty. That wasn't old, was it?

"Do you enjoy it, or does he just drag you around for the company. Fine, I remember that, 'He doesn't drag me anywhere' nonsense, but tell me honestly. Do you like him?"

"He's a good friend." I took a long sip of wine. God, was it me, or was the temperature climbing in the room. "Let's talk about something else. How's the research you were doing?"

"Sure, it's wonderful."

"Good." The heat was almost smoldering; melting my skin until a layer of sweat had formed beneath my shirt. Michael leaned forward against the table.

"Tell me, Joanna, what do you think of Ireland?"

CHAPTER TWENTY-FIVE

Thomas Patrick Keane watched as his brother, the professor, wear a line on the floorboards from his constant pacing up and down by the windows; a cigarette constantly dangling from his mouth. Every once in a while he would have to pause to light a new one, but beyond that the military thumping was beginning to make Thomas' head ache.

"Bren, do you have to do that. Watching you makes my neck stiff. I'll be looking like an old goat before long." Keane didn't stop.

"They should have been back by now. It's almost six. Six o'clock! Bloody hell, where are they."

"I'm sure they'll be barging through that door in not more than a minute. Anyroad, they're young and have years ahead of them; so, what difference would a few hours make? You remember what it was to be young, don't you, Bren?"

"I remember having to cart you home after staying out with the lads til the wee small hours. Almost had to peel that one girl off of your sorry carcass." Thomas chuckled.

"I'm surprised I didn't have to do the same for you. The lasses always liked you better." Keane shook his head and stabbed the butt of his cigarette into an already overflowing ashtray.

"Lawrence would never stay out this long without sending some word. A telephone call or something. And the snow is really coming down now. I wouldn't be the least bit shocked if it turned into a storm."

"Bren, you weren't always this much of a worry wort when we were lads. What happened?"

"What happened to Bridget?" That name, the name that had been nearly nonexistent from Keane's lips for the past few years, shot across the room with the full force of a bullet, and was twice as lethal.

"It was for her own good, Bren."

"Her own good? You damn near killed her, locking her up in that place. I could have—"

"—No, you couldn't have. That was the problem." The older brother sighed heavily as he lowered himself onto the couch. "Bren, you were only a boy. You had your own life—your own future—to think about."

"But Bridget—"

"—I know how close you two were. We all loved her. She was our sister, for feck'n sake! But she needed care, Bren. Care you were just too young to give her." Keane stopped his pacing and turned to fully face his brother, who had lowered his voice. "If it helps, I was sorry to see her go too."

A silence settled over the room, but it was light and without the normal pressures such quiet might bring. It was as though an enormous weight had been lifted from the house and all had again fallen into its proper place. There would be scars, of course, but there would always be scars; those discolored lines that, while they may sting, they also heal. Keane smiled inwardly. Lawrence would have thought something along those lines, surely. She would have sat quietly through the entire endeavor and ended it with that ever knowing grin of hers. Keane stepped again toward the window; the lines deepening on his forehead until they were jagged abysses.

Blast. Where was Lawrence?

PART FIVE

The only difference between the saint and the sinner
is that every saint has a past,
and every sinner has a future.
-Oscar Wilde

CHAPTER TWENTY-SIX

"Bren, be reasonable." Thomas chased after his younger brother, who had begun doing up the buttons to his heavy overcoat. "They're probably fine." Keane's back jerked to attention.

"Fine? It's been almost an entire day! Twenty-four hours! Look out the damn windows, Thomas, it's a bloody blizzard out there!"

"Your Joanna seemed like she had a fine head on her shoulders. She can take care of herself—"

"—I know that!" The younger brother snapped. Catherine suddenly appeared at his arm; her hand resting gently between his shoulders.

"Please, Brendan, you haven't slept all night, and if you don't eat something soon, your belly 'll think your throat was cut."

"I'm fine."

"Come on, brother, listen to Cat. Ya can't just go gallivanting out in that snowstorm. I may be older than you, but you aren't exactly young eith—"

Suddenly the door burst open in a flurry of white and wool clothing

"Good morning, Uncle. Is Joanna here?" Keane snatched the intruder by his lapels and pinned him against the closed door. It was nothing violent, but enough to make the young man squirm.

"God damn it, where is she?" Keane growled. "Michael, tell me this instant, or I swear—"

"Brendan!" Thomas pulled his brother from his son with a sharp glare. "Wait a feck'n minute and we might learn something before this becomes a feck'n boxing match. Michael, why didn't you bring Joanna back yesterday evening?" The young man brushed nervously at his coat collar.

"She said she wanted to walk back alone—had some things to think about, like—and I didn't want to get in between her and that brain of hers. Wait, you mean she didn't come back?" The dark bags under Keane's bloodshot eyes turned to hollow graves.

"No." He barked. "And, with God as my witness, if we don't find her, I'll—" This time his elder brother did not interrupt him. Rather, he stopped himself by clenching his fists until his nails etched little crescents into his palms. Damn what his brother said. There *was* a point to all his shouting. A damn good point too. Lawrence was always a damn good point. Keane flinched as Michael laid a hand on his shoulder.

"Don't worry, we'll find her quick enough. She couldn't have gone far." You don't know Lawrence, Keane thought. She could be in sunny California if she set her mind to it.

"I'll get my coat and round up some of the lads." Thomas added, but Catherine poised herself as a roadblock between her husband and the door.

"You aren't going anywhere, Thomas Francis Keane, not until Brendan gets a good hot meal in him."

What she claimed to be a hot meal escalated into a full feast of potatoes and various sorts of poultry. Keane's appetite had long since disappeared, but he managed to force down enough of the warm, heavy food to please—or at least appease—Catherine's feminine concern.

"Right," He said, pushing himself up from the kitchen table. "We'll be off then. Thomas and Michael, you get help. I will start searching."

THE WIND WHIPPED ABOUT Keane's ears and the growing snow drifts ate at his long legs. Years in the navy had done nothing to prepare him for the constant shifting of the wet snow, or the heavy white coating his clothes. It was in this, the autumn of his life, in which he faced such a winter. Entire cars had been swallowed in the storm's mighty jaws. Thick slabs of ice haunted the ground beneath a layer of white flakes. Keane kept a hand to the building at his side; wallowing in the rough brick and stone as he staggered forward along the walk.

Suddenly a slick spot grabbed his foot and jerked him to the ground with a sickening thud. What repair he had accomplished with his ribs seemed to be immediately undone in a tidal wave of immense pain and raspy breath. A hand pressed to his chest, he forced himself to sit up and prop his back against the wall. He knew where he was, even in the blinding force of the blizzard. This was the sweet shop; the last building until the world suddenly broke off into the uninhibited country. Keane sucked in a sharp breath only to find himself painting with each pained inhale burning his lungs until the spark fanned into an inferno. He coughed. Perhaps there was some truth in what Fingal had said about the new research on tobacco smoking.

He forced himself to his feet. A burning chest was far less of a danger than sitting too long. Keane steadied himself once more with a hand to the building and slowly muddling on, one step at a time. He could feel the moment the pavement ended and dirt began as he edged further into the unknown. Here there were no more walls at his fingertips' touch; no net in which he may find absolute assurance. His long legs felt as heavy as lead and cold as ice. A numbness had settled into his arms as well, but his lungs still harbored a wildfire that was stoked further with each haggard gasp. A decade ago he would not have done such a foolish thing as this. Twenty years ago he would deny any knowledge of such lack of foresight. But today he wandered the frozen world alone with only ambition keeping him dancing away from death's fingers.

He had staggered perhaps another hundred yards when he caught sight of what he feared most. A little ways off, just below a tree, the back of a leather jacket peeked out from the billowing white with the heels of brown boots edging out from the other end. Keane's stomach lurched forward against his ribs. He wanted to lie down in the white: to lie down and remain forgotten as the world so commonly makes a habit. But he did the exact opposite. He ran.

His lungs screamed against the effort when he at last dropped before the snowdrift. Swiftly he dug away at the heavy, wet pile until he pushed himself away with a strangled noise echoing from his paling lips. He plucked the jacket from the snow, folded it into a thick bundle, and tucked it securely in his own coat. It was the jacket. Only the jacket.

Keane could have jumped for joy at the relief of it all. She was alive. *Alive.* Then his spirits again plummeted as he realized it was not necessarily so. Lawrence could very well be lying face down in another drift not far away. Or very far away. She could be drowning along the coast for all he knew. As a professor it was a horrible thing to know nothing. It was almost as frightening as the two boots still peeking out of the snow. Keane knew Lawrence to be a good many things, but she was not senile. To walk through the snow without boots was an engraved invitation for frostbite or hypothermia. His fingers thickened by his gloves, he fumbled with the bootlaces until they were bound to one another and slung around his neck. Sedimentary he knew the jacket was by far more valuable, but the boots were practical. What did Keane have if not his logic. He stood, bowed his head against the wind, and slugged onward into the deadly white.

CHAPTER TWENTY-SEVEN

I awoke blind.
 I was also half frozen, stiff to the point of excruciating pain, and stinking of sweat, grime, and cold vomit. My legs—if they still existed—were completely numb and a sharp, hot knife constantly tore away at the flesh of my arms and shoulders, which had been knotted and bound around some sort of wooden pole. Even in my blindness it didn't take long to realize much of my skin was bare against the frozen floor. My legs had been stripped of their heavy trousers, leaving me in nothing but my stocking feet and undergarments beneath the thin fabric of my shirt. My leather jacket had also gone awol. I ignored the pounding in my head and managed to allow some blood to flow back to my legs, but it was scarcely a comfort. At last, I laid my head back against the pole and allowed all thought to drip from my brain.

The second time I awoke I was still blind, but not as before. Now my sight had brightened into a drunken haze blended with black against dark purple shadows. My stomach lurched constantly as a tribe of Indians pounded out their ancient ritual around my eardrums. My tongue felt thick and far too large for the rest of my mouth. Every time I tried to shout, a horse, strangled moan was the only thing to break through the silence. Soon, I just gave up and allowed sleep to again overtake me.

The third time I raised my head from the wooden pole a startling realization struck me through the thick fog. I was alive. That was something anyway, though not entirely reassuring. Yes, I was alive, but where? With the morning returned my sight, though a portion of me wished it hadn't. The pole I had been so unceremoniously bound to was a bed. More specifically, a bedpost. The mattress had also been stripped of coverings, though, unlike myself, it was not even decent. The seams were torn at the edges; frayed, if they were so fortunate. I spotted my trousers flung against the nearest wall, though my jacket was nowhere to be seen. Splinters wrenched their devilish fingers upwards between loose floorboards in what little space was left within the irritatingly close walls. Slowly I turned a critical eye toward myself.

I had not been as ill as I had thought. That is, I was without trace of vomit or malfunctions at the other end. No blood could I find pouring from some cut, no pus from an infectious wound. All was well.

And yet all was so horribly, horribly wrong.

To be face to face with the possibility of death is to recognize, not only a lack of life, but the likelihood you may soon be nothing more than a rotting corpse. From the way I was shivering I doubted I was too far from the end even without some mortal dagger slashing through my organs.

Who would even want me in such a place? I knew no one who showed any ill feelings toward me, asides some thoughtless comments about women's place in society. Any relation of mine was, to my knowledge, in the United States, and I hardly thought Keane had any enemies who were so drastic.

God, was I cold.

The wind outside howled like a thousand wolves running on a vicious hunt against some unfortunate rabbit. Suddenly I was feeling rather small, brown, and fur-covered.

Just as my mind pondered such a dreadful fate, the wooden door creaked open with the rattling of keys and a robed figure drifted in; a black robe with a hood.

He said nothing to me, but recoiled a gloved hand and slammed my head against the bedpost until my stiff, frozen body again slipped toward the darkening abyss.

WHEN I AWOKE MY HEAD had been trampled by a stampede of buffalo, mashed by heathens in the sahara, and given to King Herod on a silver platter. And yet, it was clear. For the first time in who knows how long, I was able to truly think. I thought of how I could be shot at any moment, stabbed by the man in the hood, or die of hypothermia. None were pleasant, but the last lacked any sort of dignity. My trousers still lay in a mangled heap near the wall. I wouldn't be able to put them on—I shuddered to think how red and raw my wrists would be from the rope—but I could at least use them to cover part of my bare legs. I shifted myself until I was lying on the floor and stretched my legs toward the forgotten clothing. Every snatching motion with my feet made my stomach clench and the cold, sour taste of vomit shot through my throat, but at last I felt the thick fabric between my stocking feet and pulled my knees toward my chest until the trousers dangled above me. As I did so, the quiet thud of metal snapped through the boards. A large, silver but sat by my hip.

The pocket knife.

It took a great deal of shifting, but I was at last able to clasp the object at the end of my numb fingers . . . only to drop it again when I tried to open the largest blade. After another battle, I once more held it between my fingers. Rather than immediately trying to cut the binding ropes; however, I took the silver object into my palm and allowed myself to feel the smoothness of it all. Such an insignificant thing—scarcely the size of my smallest finger—was my salvation.

CHAPTER TWENTY-EIGHT

He thought Brendan was dead. After all, a grown man hunched over a snowdrift is rarely alive. Thomas found his advancing years rebelled against a thought quite so foolish as running, so he settled for some sort of heavy gallop that turned to a staggering trudge as the snow shifted at his feet. Before he was even within a hundred yards, his brother stood and shoved something into his coat while hanging another object over his neck. Was it the hurling snow that made him look a decade older? Certainly a few hours in the storm wasn't enough to make him appear quite *that* old. Was it?

Thomas struggled up to his brother's shoulder.

"Anything yet?" He almost had to shout in Brendan's ear to be heard above the thrashing winds. Brendan pulled open the top of his coat to reveal a bunched up sleeve of a leather RAF jacket.

"How far is it to the country house?" Thomas grabbed his brother's sleeve.

"You're feck'n mad. At least wait back at the house until the storm lets up."

"It won't do any good for me to be huddled up beside a warm fire while she freezes out there."

"And it won't help her one speck more if you end up face down in a ditch." Brendan jerked his arm away from Thomas' grasp. Face down in a ditch indeed.

"How many men did you find? Are there enough for a search party?"

"If you count all the drunks, we could have five parties."

"And without them?"

"You, me, Michael, Fingal, and only a handful of others." Brendan sighed. Then he nodded his head fervently.

"It's not much, but it's enough. When can we start?"

"Not until tomorrow."

"Lawrence might not be able to wait that long!" Thomas again tried to grab his brother's sleeve, but this time Brendan avoided it by crossing his arms over his chest. Thomas did the same.

"Brendan, has it occurred to you that she might be sitting in front of the fire in some cottage, safe and sound?"

"And if she isn't?" Neither brother cared to consider that option, though the likelihood was far higher than either would dare admit. Brendan's voice grew low, near inaudible. "Thomas, she doesn't know this land like you or I. She has only seen a small glimmer of the ponds and cliffs in this area. You once told me Bridget died by drowning after she fell through some thin ice. What keeps Lawrence from suffering the same fate?"

"But Bridget was sent to a hospital. The ice was just a story."

"With Lawrence it could damn well be true." Keane barked. What was it she had quoted from *King Lear*? Something about legitimacy. This was as legitimate a situation if ever he knew one.

Thomas uncrossed his arms and began the useless task of brushing the snow from his coat. With every one snowflake he banished, a hundred more flew against him. It was not long before he gave up.

"True or not, we can't do a thing about it this late in the day. We'll start out first thing tomorrow."

CHAPTER TWENTY-NINE

It must have been tomorrow, or at least some time after yesterday. The darkness outside screamed and wailed constantly. I was going mad. I knew it. Then again, a person who has truly lost all logical sense is rarely able to notice its disappearance. Perhaps I was not mad then. But what was I? I began to review my situation for the hundredth time.

I had managed to open my blade—with a few scratches to my person—and cut away the ropes until I was at last able to draw my hands in front of me. My wrists had indeed rubbed raw from the mistreatment, and my fingers did look a bit pale, but else they were unharmed. Somehow I was able to fold my legs back under me into a predatory crouch.

Standing was like pushing a stubborn mule up a hill when it was bound and determined to go the other way. The fog in my head thickened, my legs snapped, the room whirled. A sickening knot wrenched inself into my stomach with a mighty growl. How long had it been since last I had eaten? Too long—far too long—by the sounds of it.

But I wouldn't think about that now. I oughtn't, for it would do me no good.

My head was struck mightily with every hot, burning pulse of my heart and the only thing keeping my fractured form from tumbling back to the frozen floor was a hand gripping the wooden bedpost. I stretched my right leg first. The skin was scraped at the knee, as well as several angry red patches spotting my calf. The left leg was much the same, save a long, jagged scratch at my ankle. It was nothing too worrisome, but working the trousers over my battered lower half was like a seasick sailor in a hurricane. With each jerk of the fabric my stomach lurched and threatened to upheave its emptiness onto the sea of splintered wood. At last the tweed trousers were buttoned securely at my waist, though the belt was missing.

There was a hole in my left stocking, something I had certainly not noticed before. But now it bit into my toes like a shark. My stomach again began to tremble with hunger. What was the Irish saying?

Belly thinks the throat's been cut.

Not only cut, I thought, but missing an entire head. My throat too was thickly caked with dust and grime.

What butter and whiskey cannot cure—

I lowered my right foot in the first attempt at what may tentatively be called a step. My leg seemed to snap beneath me, but it wasn't quite so threatening as when I had climbed to my feet. I took another step. Then another. Than another.

After about a half an hour (I still, thank God, had my wristwatch) I was pacing the long side of the room with, slow, carefully measured steps. The room rocked and pitched as I did so, but eventually the seas calmed and I was at last master at the helm.

My stomach let out a low growl.

—cannot be cured.

I tried the door. Locked. For some odd reason my mind almost seemed surprised at this. I slowly squatted down—fearing a mutiny of my legs—and peered through the keyhole. It wasn't anything outstanding. It wasn't even complicated. I could pick it in a minute. Two, if I took into account my sorry state.

I pulled the screwdriver bit from my multitool and was just about to stick it through when the scream of a front door was followed by the eerie thud of footsteps. My fingers shoved the bit back into place and replaced it with the longest blade tucked in the silver cover. It was shorter than my thumb, but it was enough. I stealthily clambered to the corner just as the wicked cackle of keys tightened the knot in my stomach.

As soon as the hooded figure had fully entered the room, I lept upon it with all my strength and slashed downward with my knife. An ice cold scream darted between the walls as I felt the small but mighty blade meet the flesh of its robed arm. A hot, thick substance poured onto my hands and down my newly trousered legs. The figure's untouched arm flailed outward and caught my jaw. I had the distinct feeling that I had taken flight before landing backwards on the floor. My head snapped as it had so many times in the last few hours, but this was not quite so threatening as before. For a long moment I lay sprawled, stunned, and increasingly aware of a sharp pain in my neck. The hooded ghost stepped over me and grabbed the shirt at my neck, withdrawing a gloved hand that was level with my nose. Again I lashed forward, but this time with clenched fists until at last the figure slackened and folded onto the floor.

I slipped the knife back into my pocket, grabbed the keys, scurried out of the room, and locked the door behind me. Cold air surged into my lungs; stoking a burning that worsened with every breath. My bottom lip felt wet and thick with the taste of iron dripping onto my tongue. The skin along my jaw was tattered and painfully rough to the touch of my pale fingers, as was the area surrounding my left eye. No doubt a great number of bruises would appear in the next few hours.

But I was free.

The room in which I was now standing had been striped bare of carpets, furniture, and most any other domestic pieces that might have existed at some point in its life. The splintering floorboards only ended where grey, chipped paint began; climbing up the walls until they too came to an abrupt halt at the ceiling. The windows had been covered by the faded, thin shreds of paper; separating what little light there was into enormous claws groping along the floor. Near the corner there was a small crate of tattered clothing and ancient boots. I shuffled through these and dressed myself in what seemed the best fit. Even so, the sweater still sagged emptily at my waist and I had to shove a filthy sock into each boot before they fit, but I was warm. Or at least it was an improvement.

There was also a chair and table with a few megre scraps of bread and cheese. My stomach lurched forward at the sight. I took out my knife and carved away the grey bits and shoved what was left into my mouth before washing it all down with a few swigs of old whiskey left in a bottle. More satisfied than I had been for more than a day, my body yawned and stretched. But to sleep would have been as foolish a thing as anyone in my position might have done. I dug around the crate once more and pulled from it the patched remains of a dirt-infested overcoat. The sleeves were torn and frayed to the wrists, but it fit over the whiskey-stained sweater and that was enough.

I slunk sluggishly toward the door, well aware of how large the borrowed clothes were on my feminine frame. Outside the wind's howels had heightened to deafening screams as the world was white without so much as a shadow of other color. A dull, dismal grey overcast the skies in a gloom shared only by a battalion of soldiers trudging wearily onward through the enemy's land. Only a fool would go out in such a blizzard, I thought with a heavy sigh.

Oh, what a fool was I.

IN JUST A FEW DAYS the entire world had become a snowglobe; one of those Christmas ornaments that, upon being shaken, resorted to the chaos of a million snowflakes dropping like lead and carried upon a thousand different currents. With the blizzard came nature's determination to rid itself of all those foolhardy enough to test its wrath. And the primal force was willing to batter my bones in all possible ways until all its energy had been released. I staggered onward from forests of bowling green to sheets of pure white stabbing at my face.

It hadn't entirely occurred to me I knew not where I was going, just as it made no difference how long I walked as I had no sense of which direction I took. All the landmarks I had made note of on my walks with Keane had dissipated into the white madness, though, as I hardly knew the house from which I started, it would have made no difference. I only knew I must keep moving—keep walking—else the icy winds that made my bones tremble stop them completely. I edged onward. I dragged my legs through the swamps of snow and the marshes of ice.

There were more flakes than I could ever count, even if I had all the time in the world. Just as I began to follow a single white speck it was bashed by another and flew off in a different direction completely. The snow was so thick the trees looked like decrepit old men, bowing low against the haggard winds. The rocks lurking in front of me were little more than dim outlines of gaunt faced leering at me. These flecks of ice I had found almost bewitching behind a pane of glass now packed down my neck and the flaps of fabric left open at the front. Winter's icy hands groped at my neck; strangling life from me just as assuredly as brother death would throw me headlong into a ditch. But sister earth was far the smartest of them all. In a matter of seconds, she had twisted her fingers around my ankles and dragged me facedown in the snow. I leveled my arms and shoved upward with all my might, but nothing happened. A fresh layer of winter's ice had covered my back and weighted my head down against the soft pillow of snow. It *was* soft; softer than any bed in which I had slept. Its heavy arms rocked and comforted be just as the wind quieted to a whispered lullaby.

No. I should get up. I *must* get up.

But oh what a welcome feeling it was to feel my legs stop shivering and the violent ache in my stomach to unwind into a warm, blissful calm.

No. For God's sake, Lawrence, get up! To your feet, damn it! To your feet!

How long had it last been since I slept; truly slept? Too long. Much too long. I could just close my eyes for a moment. Just fifty winks. Surely that would be alright.

Damn it, Lawrence, where's your strength? Get up! What would Keane think if he saw—

Keane.

I hadn't thought of him for quite some time, and yet he had never drifted too far from my mind. He seldom did. What would he say if he saw me lying in this ditch? No doubt he would feel some remorse, but his life would continue on. His life always did. He had always been that stubborn, prideful person. The walls of Jerico could have tumbled down at his feet and he would have merely stepped over the rubble. Had was no doubt one of the men who would have stood his post as the Titanic sunk beneath the ocean's thrashing waves. Were he American (and about sixty years older) there was no doubt he would have held his ground like Davy Crocket at the Alamo.

Yes, Lawrence, yes! What would Keane say if he found you like this? What would he say? What would he do?

I sighed and slowly closed my eyes. Frankly, I was too exhausted to give a damn.

CHAPTER THIRTY

I awoke gradually without fully knowing I had fallen asleep. The world seemed to have begun moving beneath me.

No, wait, the earth wasn't moving, *I* was. More specifically, I was being carried. I forced open one eye and found myself staring up at a tall, grey-haired man.

"Keane?" I muttered, a slow smile warming my frozen face. "God, Keane, you sure took your time." My head was ruffled with a deep chuckle as I nodded back into a warming darkness.

It must have been some time before I awoke again; because, the entire world had changed. The snow ridden skies had been replaced by an old wood ceiling and floral wallpaper that peeled slightly at the edges. There was a bed again, but this time I was in it, rather than bound to it. My limbs were surrounded by a cloud of linen sheets topped with a patchwork quilt made of greens, whites, and pleasant browns. On the table at my side was a pitcher and glass of water, along with the contents of my pockets; my knife, a lighter, and a pack of cigarettes I kept around in case Keane ran out of his own. (Which seemed to be a constant occurrence lately.)

Near the end of the room was a quaint stone fireplace that had been stoked recently and crackled with warmth and merriment. Next to that was a wooden door. Open.

"Good morning to you." I jerked up in the bed to find a woman stationed in a wooden chair to my right. I also realized my clothes had been taken. Again. This time, thank God, they had been replaced by a wool nightshirt that would easily hang down to my knees if I were standing. Beyond that, nothing. I tugged the quilt up to my collarbone and faced the woman next to me. She wasn't a bad looking woman. In fact, she was quite beautiful. Thick locks of chocolate hair curled to her shoulders in long, well-kept ringlets around a simple but pretty face. The green dress she was wearing pleasantly offset her watery-blue eyes and brought out the soft pink glow in her cheeks. Her skin was fair and accentuated her square-jawed cheek bones until they stood out as another prominent feature just above a set of lips that might have been considered a tad too small. I would have thought her a fine thirty-five, though I suspected she was a bit older.

"Good morning." I whispered, the words scratching painfully at my throat. The woman rose in a rustle of skirts and female flippery as she bustled to the other side of the bed and handed me the glass.

"Sure, you must be dry as the Sahara. Drink this down, and you'll soon be right again." I took the offering and forced myself to slowly sip the sweet water, rather than down the entire thing. "It was my husband who found you out in the snow, thank God. Carried you back here he did, like the stories of Jesus and the lost lamb."

"Matthew 18:12." The woman smiled. She had a very nice, kind smile. The edges of her thin lips turned upward and caused her blue eyes to twinkle slightly.

"Ye know the Bible? Sure I shouldn't be too surprised, but, by the sounds of your voice I would think you an American."

"That I am, and a Catholic too." I didn't add that a Catholic church in England was about as hard to find as a handful of marbles in an African desert; they existed somewhere, but were damn difficult to find. I held out my hand. "My name's Joanna Lawrence. Jo, for short." The woman shook my hand; a surprisingly strong grasp for someone who looked so fragile.

"Pleased to meet you, Jo. I'm Fiona. Now, if you'll be excusing me, I'll heat some hot soup for your breakfast. Sure, it's lucky my Sean found you when he did. A poor soul could catch pneumonia out in that storm." Not to mention hypothermia, frostbite, and a good many others, I added mentally as she left the room. It seemed like only a matter of seconds before she came bustling back with a spoon clinking cheerily in a simple, white bowl. As she set it on the table, she took one long look at the pack of cigarettes lying idly on the polished wood.

"You shouldn't be smoking. It's bad for your lungs, so. I read an article about it just a day or two ago, so I did. Said it makes it hard to breathe."

"It's my friend who smokes, not me, though I think he could use your lecture with the way he empties those cartons." The woman brushed aside the symbol of evil habits and set the bowl down in its stead.

"Sure, let's not go talking of unhappy things. Eat up that soup and I might make up some toast if you feel up to it. Mind you don't bolt it like." I thanked Fiona, who smiled again and turned toward the door.

"Oh, may I ask a question?" She stopped and turned back toward me. "Where are my clothes?"

"Sure, I had to get rid of the lot of them. Blood all over them and smelling of whiskey like. Don't ye worry, when you're strong enough you can wear some of mine. Now, eat up before it gets cold." That was one order I could follow very well.

I STAYED IN BED FOR the first day and a half after I woke up, but by the second day I was ready to again be a part of the world. True to her word, Fiona lent me some of her old clothes; a pair of scuffed boots, wool socks, and denim overalls I wore over one of her husband's old work shirts.

Fiona's husband was a man somewhat changed from what I saw of him out in the blizzard. His features told of a man somewhere either late in his forties or early fifties. The snow had exaggerated the grey in his hair, which was really just a little tuff at his temples before spreading into a fiery shock of red hair. His exceptionally low voice, matched with his strong vice grip, nearly tore me limb from limb when he shook my hand. His face, which was constantly drawn into a broad grin, had weathered the years with a crimson hue that colored his cheeks and the tips of his ears. At some point in his life he must have been a boxer, or a man of some other violent sport, as his ears were of the infamous cauliflower variety tucked neatly against his head of vivid hair.

Sean and Fiona were the sort of married pair in which their differences were played together into a rather amusing pair. When they stood together Fiona looked infinitely small and petite against her husband's well-fed frame, a subject that appeared conspicuously during dinner one evening.

"Sean, you keep your hands off of that lamb. You've no doubt eaten enough to keep an army on its feet for days." The large man grinned impishly.

"Sure, but isn't the thing cooked to be eaten? Seems an awful shame to let it go to waste."

"It's not the lamb's waist I'm worried about." Fiona retorted with a glance to her husband's soft middle. "Now, if you'll pull out a bottle of something nice, Sean, I think we ought to have a little party to raise our morale. Sure, isn't it grand to have a little party now and again? We have some records shipped in from America last year and—no, better yet—Sean, me darl'n, once you're through getting the cork off that, would you mind playing a tune on your violin? Something lively, mind you." Her husband popped the cork off a bottle of Jameson, handed out the glasses, and went over to a worn case propped up in the corner. It was a handsome looking instrument if ever I saw one; dark wood polished to a sparkling gleam and a bow without bend or fault. He tucked the violin under his chin and swung the bow casually between his fingers.

"What'll it be then? I play a grand Swallowtail when in the mind for it." Fiona clapped her hands together, as if all the world's problems would be solved in that one slap of her palms.

"Sure, why don't you make something up like and we'll dance to it. You do know how to dance, don't you Jo? Sure, it's nothing too difficult. I'll show you how it's done." In a matter of moments, and a few clumsy lessons, I was following her lead as she leapt, jumped, and stepped in time with Sean's skipping bow. Fiona's laugh, for it was indeed just as light of a laugh as a carefree child, bubbled up to the ceiling before drifting back down as shimmering dust that bestowed a gradure about the entire event. The simple blue curtains transformed to red velvet. Her dress whirled and sparkled with every spin of her heels. The famous Irish whiskey flowed freely from the bottle, and more often into Sean's glass than not. The already reddish hue of his face tinged further as his smile broadened and his bow leapt more dangerously from the different strings. Even the ceiling itself, which was bare, held decorations of the finest paper and flowered vines one associates with the fresh bounds of spring. All was in its proper place with a thousand times more beauty than a stranger would imagine peeking through a window, far more than the infamous fly on the wall could even witness. The music grew and swelled with every measured step until there seemed nothing else in the world but that moment, tucked safely away in the little cottage.

JUST AS SEAN PAUSED his bow to take a sip of whiskey, a pounding erupted upon the door and sent out little illusion crashing down around our feet. The velvet curtains fell away from the blue. Fiona's dress became green. Even the paper decorations retreated into the hard, splinter-infested wood. And the world once again tumbled into reality.

Fiona rushed to the window near the door and gasped.

"Jesus, Mary, and Joseph! Sean, open the door, the man's half frozen out there. I'll put on the tea." As she scuttled off in a whisper of skirts, her husband lay his violin aside and swung open the door in a single bound. The man who staggered in looked hardly a man behind the cocoon of wool and leather. His hat had been tied down with a scarf and the pack strapped to his back gave the iminent reminder of Quasimodo. As I stepped forward to take the hunch from his back, I was suddenly pulled forward against the man in something that might have been called a warm embrace if I were not suddenly wet and cold. My initial reaction was a practical one; give him a good punch in the gut and see what he has to say then. However, my instinct took over and I wrapped my arms securely around his shoulders and drank in the frozen, but still existent scents, of tobacco. The hands at my back trembled.

"God, Keane, you're shivering. Here, get out of those wet things." The second phrase was said in the disillusionment the task would be a simple one. Far from it. As I peeled away stripps of soddon wool, Keane's familiar face appeared before me with a mass of unruly curls plastered down with snow in a thousand different directions, none of them natural. His face dripped with icy sweat that had frozen into his eyebrows, adding flecks of white to the grey. His cheeks were pink from the cold where his normal pallor had always been. Really, it he looked rather dignified, quite stately, rather—CRASH!

Fiona stood surrounded by the lifeless body of a once majestic teacup. Her eyes had glazed over in a blue fog and a thin hand was raised over her mouth. Before any of us had the chance to react, she was bounding across the room and throwing herself against Keane with her arms thrown wide.

Never had I been so blind.

PART SIX

If youth knew; if age could.
-Sigmund Freud

CHAPTER THIRTY-ONE

Keane sat on the edge of the sofa nearest the fireplace, his soaking, ice-infested clothes replaced by a thick wool sweater and tweed trousers, both considerably larger than his slim figure. His sister curled into his side more like a child than a woman. Sean had wedged himself into a cushioned armchair with what was left of the whiskey between his hands, while Keane's teacup rested idly on his knee. The snow had melted, leaving his hair damp and curling at his ears and the dark lines under his eyes warned of a harrowing journey with nary sleep enough to lift him from the sofa. He was smiling however, looking far more at peace than I had seen in many weeks. When he spoke, exhaustion had sanded some of the clip from his well accentuated consonants, but there was such warmth in his words that might easily drone the most mighty of lions into a gentle rest. Had it really been only an hour or so earlier when he reluctantly broke away from the woman—Fiona—and grinned at me with more joy than any sober man should be allowed.

"Lawrence, may I present my sister: Bridget Fiona Keane." How humiliating it is not to know a thing until it stands right in front of you with a hand offered in friendship. I shook her small hand as though it was the first moment of our acquaintance, rather than the fact we had just been dancing around the room like wild banshees. Their eyes were their anchoring trait; deep pools of silvery-blue shimmering on the lake of aged existence. Keane's rarely demonstrative nature served as the counterbalance for Brigit's seemingly constant attachment to him.

As I watched the two sitting on the sofa, her hand remained in his like a child who had just found a long lost friend. In many ways she was a child.

Her features reflected a lasting youth, just as her green dress had been cut more for a girl than a woman. Her manners reflected a graceful femininity only the tricks of time could supply, and yet it had not drained the true appreciation of life only a child could truly understand.

SEAN HAD TAKEN HIS wife to bed and I had migrated to the chair facing Keane. The snow had not let up in the slightest, nor had the wind's deafening growl softened. It didn't seem to matter anymore. Keane had long since finished his tea and had begun a small glass of whiskey in its stead.

"Does it surprise you?" I paused and began again. "Does it surprise you she married her doctor?" Keane's deep chuckle floated to my ears.

"Not in the slightest. Bridget may be many things, but her logic has always been impeccable."

"Just like her brother?" Keane stared into the liquor and the edges of his mouth darted upwards.

"'*Compliments pass when the quality meet.*'"

"Brendan Behan." My companion grinned, closed his eyes, and settled back into the sofa's plush surface. He looked so peaceful, almost like the young boy I had learned so much about the past month. It seemed such a shame to disturb him, and yet—

"Keane, about the last few days," I breathed deeply and paused that the words might miraculously fall into place. They didn't. Keane; however, seemed much more prepared.

"Michael told me you wished to walk back by yourself, though I would have thought your sense of direction was far better than this." The second part was a jest, but his voice was completely bereft of its usual lightness. His eyes caught mine so intently I felt obliged to stride across the room and sit beside him. Those thin, agile fingers slowly pushed me forward until my nose was mere inches above my knees. I felt hair brushed away from the nape of my neck and his cool touch brushing over a retreating lump I hadn't known of until that moment. His thumb wandered higher along my skull, above my ears, and over my temples. Finally, his hands were again clasped together in his lap as I gradually sat back up. When he spoke again, he voice was incredibly controlled and dry of all phonetic mannerisms I had labeled completely as his own.

"Do you have headaches?"

"Not anymore."

"Nausea?"

"No."

"Let me see your eyes." I shifted on the sofa until I was facing Keane. Again his hands were raised, the palms cupping the sides of my face as his fingers tactfully positioned my line of sight that I was staring directly up at him.

How blue his eyes were. Of course, I had noticed this a million times, but not once could I look at him without seeing those watery oceans drawing me to their depth. They were always so familiar, so comforting, almost like a book you know almost by memory, but read it over again all the same.

His fingers again stretched forward and pushed back a few wisps of my hair before immediately returning to the whiskey he had abandoned on the side table.

"I think you'll pull through alright, but I'll have Fingal take a look at you when we get back." Keane downed the last contents of his glass and stood. "Now, to bed with you."

"Come now, Keane, you can't order me about like a child. Besides, I think it would be best if you took the spare bed tonight." My companion's shoulders shot back indignantly.

"Good God, Lawrence," He muttered. "I may be many things, but I am not as decrepit as you seem to believe."

"No, it's not that." Sailors beware the waters already rough to the helm, for the worst shall come before the calm. "It's just I thought—"

"I know what you thought." Keane replied quickly before that gentle smile crept across his exhausted features and his voice fell to the low hum of a ship's engine as it steered a course all of its own. "I appreciate the settlement, but either bed or sofa—or even the floor—it doesn't matter. I'd be happy with anything dry and warm."

"Good. Take the bed."

"Lawrence—"

"Take. The. Bed. I'm shorter and would be more comfortable on the sofa." I expected some dignified argument, some verbose blanket woven from years of gentlemanly conduct. More than that, I waited impatiently for words that would taunt my mind until I believed myself on the brink of victory, only to awaken the next morning with the rueful knowledge I had been tricked. Much to my shock and consternation, neither of these weapons did he choose. Rather he took my hand in his and appeared to examine my palms with long, light strokes of his thumb. Just as I was about to jerk it away to the safety of my pockets, he raised it, brushed it with his cool lips, let go, and gave me a gentle shove toward the guest room door. While my mind reeled in a thousand directions, my feet worked marvelously and brought me to the edge of the mattress with a soft sigh of springs.

It wasn't until the world announced morning's approach I came to myself with a start and found I had again fallen prey to the careful play of life's chess pieces, each skillfully maneuvered by Keane.

Damn the man.

THERE WAS LITTLE ENOUGH to do over the next few days, but such a time felt like a drop in the sea in comparison to the long years

Keane and Bridget had spent apart. Sean McCladah was every bit as dedicated as my companion to their shared profession. Often, when Bridget wasn't clinging to her brother's shirtsleeves, the two men would smoke and discuss the theories tossed about from the great minds of Europe. To them it was as much an art as Beethoven and Bach.

What was it Doyle once said? Something about art in the blood?

Whatever it was, it was shared equally between the siblings; however, where I had often seen it reflected in Keane's work, or, on those rare occasions, photography, Bridget seemed entirely satisfied to sit cross legged on a shag of carpet and sketch. First it was a teacup, then a loaf of bread, then Keane's reading glasses lying on a book of poetry, then Keane himself. All were as great a reflection of life as Keane's photographs, black and white representations of a moment soon to be long past and little more than a cloud of mist drifting over a sea of what had once been. To our little foursome, life became as near to faultless domestication as one can possibly get without a large, drooling dog sleeping at your feet. But even domesticity can fall prey to impatience.

"Jesus, Mary, and Joseph, sit still Bren or sure I won't get your nose just so."

"Damn my nose." Keane muttered as he again took up the inhuman posture dictated by Bridget's charcoal pencil. She lifted the said object from the thick sketching paper with a long, entirely feminine seigh.

"Sure, but it's a grand nose. A Roman nose, to be sure. Wouldn't you agree, Jo?" My head shot up from the book open in my lap, reasonably startled by a question no policeman would ever ask.

"I can't say I've ever thought about it." Keane grunted, but he could never fully conceal that pompous air that often flitted about his head like his own personal halo.

"Sure, but it is a grand nose." Bridget sighed again as she at last relinquished her brush with a few final strokes near the center of the paper. "Done. How do ya like it?" Keane stiffly rose from the wooden chair, stretched, and ambled lazily over behind his sister.

Sister.

With every breath I was still scarce to believe it. This woman who had used her middle name for a fresh start was the very sister who inspired my companion's unusual profession. It felt entirely unreal, and yet I could have expected nothing less from the world.

Silver glasses propped up on his nose, Keane examined the painting with his customary low chuckle.

"By God," He smiled. "Do I really look that old?" Bridget stiffened indignantly.

"I think you look distinguished." And indeed she was right.

The soft, grey lines of his hair turned dark as they neared his ears and long face. A few strokes of pencil created laugh-lines dancing away from a pair of twinkling eyes. Bridget had captured them perfectly and without flaw, just as the true subject seemed entirely without fault. The irises shined bright against the fading charcoal with as much light as the sun upon its early rising or a platoon of stars resting in a formation too glorious to truly comprehend. The dark lines of exhaustion had vanished as though they had never stolen so much as a breath from so stately a man. The edge of his chin was rightly set with more life than God seemingly intended for any mere mortal. Were Keane "mere" in anything, I might have thought it a scandal, a horrible cheat to those of us whose place in Heaven was not yet reserved. As for the rest of his face, it had been represented with the same iconic vigor; those lasting expressions of youth toned and deepened with the sands of time.

Keane grinned and slowly began to tuck away his silver glasses. It was entirely him. Entirely and fully as the world seemed to rest solely upon his fingertips. To most every human being such a task would, at best, be daunting. Yet to him it seemed never to be so. I watched as he strode across the room with those quick, masterful steps swallowing the floor with a rolling gait matched by any merchant seaman. He gathered a cigarette from his pocket, put it to his lips, burnt the end, then began to leisurely fill the room with that bitter smoke that brought such comfort to him. Yes, I thought of these things quite often, not possessive as though they were my own, but with the same fondness as one would have for a wild dog. Though it be free, and often unpredictable, an attachment is formed.

But was I "in love" with him?

Ridiculous. The thought was instantly dismissed into that darkened area in all minds.

And yet—

And yet it shook me to the very core, sparks shooting down my spine with an odd, tingling sensation. Of course I couldn't be in love with him.

But why not?

The doubts and frenzies of a heated passion had never crossed my mind, and most certainly not his. Ours was a relationship—a *friendship*—cooled beneath the vast lakes of knowledge and calmed by years of professional association stiffened with a shared intelect. He was my editor, my most hated critic, my most admired support, my greatest friend.

But did I love him?

Ah, now there in lay the realms of technicality, for where fiery passions were not so much as the faintest glimpse of a spark, there was some connection that ran deep between our lives.

Love, however. Deep, comfortable, concerned love was, I thought a different matter entirely.

Were I to strip myself of all self-delusions, to toss them readily aside as the world had with logic and compromise, I would realize I did love Keane. That I had loved him far longer than anyone else who had made an appearance in my life. I had never been one for unbridled passions or illogical bouts of romanticism, but what is one to believe when they have drawn themselves so securely to another human being that they have created anything other than one of the greatest loves—perhaps the only love—they would see in their lifetime.

It wasn't some droll play of femininity. It was a fact; a cold, hard, wonderful fact completely bereft of flowers, chocolates, and idle dribble that was worth little more than a risque novel bought at a penny and dime store. It was a different sort of love, a respect that ran far deeper than mere emotion. It was worth a thousand times more than gold, while retaining all the fine repute of a sharp cut diamond. We were two separate units, and considered ourselves as such, and yet there was no denying some finer existence.

But if that was so, what was this odd sensation I felt toward Michael?

CHAPTER THIRTY-TWO

"Keane, why the hell don't you just tell me?" My companion calmly lowered the book to his lap and peered up at me through his reading glasses.

"I beg your pardon?"

"You heard me. There's something on your mind you aren't telling me and I want you to spit it out. *Now*."

"Lawrence, I make it a point never to 'spit out' anything. I was merely thinking." And Hitler was merely a bad person.

I took in Keane's utter control with no end of frustration. Damn the man. He looked so distinguished reclining on the sofa, his legs resting on the cushions with the ankles crossed over each other. So—so damn dignified. My fingers clenched and it was all I could do not to pummel him with a series of well-trained punches. It may not improve the situation in the long run, but it would certainly make me feel much better now.

Where there is only a choice between cowardice and violence, I would advise violence.

But this was not cowardice. This was fury. Hot, burning, wild fury. I took a step toward him, raised my fists, and collapsed into a nearby armchair. When the time came to fight, I was more than ready, but it was against all rules of gentlemen and fighters to attack when the other party was reading. (Or in my opinion, anyway.) Keane brought down this wall; however, as he slowly shut the book, placed it on the side table, and laid the silver reading glasses on top of it.

"And how is your head today, Lawrence?"

"Damn my head." Damn my head. Damn his nose. Damn it all. Damn.

Keane removed his feet from the couch and patted the new empty space beside him. Like a defeated warrior, I obeyed and was again subjected to the humiliating process of being pushed forward as his fingers wandered along the nape of my neck and bottom of my skull. His skin was cool against my face as he examined my temples, then just behind my ears, then finally my eyes. Once more satisfied he gave a little hum of approval and reached for his abandoned book.

"Good. You seem to be healing well. Always remember, Lawrence, *'The mind is not a vessel to be filled, but a fire to be kindled.'*" I fought the urge to roll my eyes.

"I'll write that in my 'Things to Remember' book this very night." Keane scoffed cooly and settled back into his book: *Swiss Family Robinson*. It was a book I had read many times, but not, I thought, something on his literary list. When I said as much; however, he gave that warm chuckle and ran the palm of his hand over the worn, faded cover before placing it in my hands.

"Look inside." I did as I was told and found a piece of paper that had torn and yellowed at the edges, but, beyond that, the script was clear. I blinked twice and realized I had read that same script, albeit an older, more refined variation, a thousand times in the papers strewn about Keane's desk. My mouth formed neatly around the spidery words, my tongue lapping at the syllables foreign to my mind.

When I had finished, my companion kindly translated the words of his youth into his deep English clip, the sin of all Irishman and the glory of my ears.

"*If God made me a rover*
And I wandered forein shores
My gun I would relinquish
If all of life be yours.
And if God made me a soldier

Let the men call me a cad
I can't pull that hated trigger
To kill the other lad
And if God made me a priest
And I walked among the dead
I'd rather be lying with them
Than bowing o're their head
But God made me a man
Be there you or there be I
One of us will perish
And stare up at the sky."

When Keane's voice struck the final line, it vibrated up to the rafters and broke among the wood only to fall in shattered pieces around my ears. It stole the breath from my lungs, pilched the dry from my eyes, and poured the blood of a million men onto my battered soul. I sat back, stunned for a long moment that seemed to stretch and grow into a thousand years. Somehow the paper was returned to my hands—Did my fingers always tremble so?—and I folded it along the yellowing creases and returned it to the inside cover of the book.

When at last my voice came, it came as little more than a whisper that floated wearily through the air just as lost as the passing time.

"I've never heard that poem before."

"I should say not." Keane muttered. He tapped the hard book cover with his forefinger. "I wrote that dribble back in my navy days. A man needed to do anything he could not to think about tomorrow or the day after. To do otherwise would drive you stark staring mad." I said nothing, but sat silently as he sharply inhaled. "When you spend your days on the same ship as a hundred shell-shocked sailors, it is impossible for some of it not to rub off on you. Do you know, for more than a year after I was discharged, I couldn't even look at a gun? Even the sound—" Keane fingered the edge of the book, his hands brushing mine as he did so. "I believe our murderer is much the same."

"You think he has shell-shock?"

"It's the only logical explanation. Three out of four times there has been some kind of firearm nearby, but he—or she—has taken great pains to avoid their use. They may; however, use it as a last resort." My spine tingled lightly as his thumb passed lightly over the side of my wrist.

"But the boy—"

"Yes, that also caused me some consternation. Remember that fairy story you were so opposed to? Think, Lawrence, think. What sort of boy would go out in the woods and search for mythical creatures often attributed to female interests?" My eyes shot open.

"God, Keane, you don't think—"

"That he was schizophrenic? We must consider it a possibility."

"And the women; Agatha Brown, Eileen O'Brian, and—did you ever learn that other woman's name?" Keane's hands dove for his cigarette case.

"I did. It was Joan Kelly. Curran was her son's."

"So, between Brown, O'Brian, and Kelly, they had all been involved in earning tainted money at some point in their life. And if Curran *was* a schizophrenic..." I paused. It all seemed so unreal—so ludicrous—it might just be true. "Keane, is it possible someone is trying to 'weed out the undesirables'?" The cigarette bobbed in his mouth.

"Possible? Lawrence, such actions have echoed through the world since the jealousy of Cain and Abel. Humanity has come up with everything from the Druids to the Klu Klux Klan. We just fought a war against a mass dictator, for God's sake. Will we never learn?" Keane tore the half-smoked cigarette from his mouth and banished it into the fireplace with one, mighty sweep of his arm. His eyes blazed just as mightily as the flames lapping greedily at the oxygen around us, stealing our breath and draining our life.

"It is as Socrates said," I ventured cautiously. "'*There is only one good, knowledge, and one evil, ignorance.*'"

"Are you familiar with central African tribes? No?" Keane held a match to the end of a fresh cigarette and snuffed it out with a few quick flicks of his wrist. "Some tribes pride themselves on cooperation with one another in peaceful tranquility. Now, to you and I this may sound rather idealistic, but it works for them. Other tribes; however, are built upon a jealousy and violence that is instilled upon them at a tender age. Brother is pinned against brother until they are all forced to live separately with miles of empty space between them. If any stranger would dare try to visit this tribe . . . I take it you have heard of headhunters? If you were different, well . . ." The hair on the back of my neck leapt to attention. Keane took a long, somber draw of his cigarette, settled onto the sofa once more, and shifted around that his eyes towered above me. Blue though they were, somewhere in our conversations a cold grey had begun the fight for control. I was aware of his hand running over mine in something far more abhorrent than simple comfort.

Concern.

"Lawrence, I need you to tell me everything from the moment you left Michael to when I walked through that door. And, by God, I do mean anything."

"I am not one of your patients." I tugged my hand from his grasp, but his fingers did not bother to follow. Instead, they folded themselves neatly in his lap.

"No, no you're not. Nor are you a fish, nor bird, nor rabbit—must I go on? Come now, I know you far too well for this childish behavior." He did know me too well. He knew that I trusted him infinitely, and that was enough. I sighed. Damn the man.

"Fine. I awoke in a room—I don't know what room or in what house—that was infinitely small. I had been tied to a bedpost and—" Keane leapt up, his eyes bulging slightly, his cheekbones almost purple, and his ears singeing red. He didn't seem to know what to do with his hands as they jerked in and out of his pockets, flew at his precious cigarettes, and eventually settled by accentuating his every word.

"By God, he didn't force—by God, if he did I'll kill him! I'll—"

"For heaven's sake, Keane, sit down before you have a heart attack. No, he did *not* take advantage of me. Merely bashed me around a bit was all, but I also gave him a nice cut on his arm. Thank you for that pocketknife, by the way." My companion said nothing but collapsed heavily into an armchair, the springs protesting the sudden attack. For a long moment there was little more than the howl of the wind and I was tempted to tell Keane how I had first thought Sean to be him out in that snowstorm.

How I *hoped* it was him.

But I found I could not force my—yes, I shall admit it—emotions to complete so strenuous a task. It was rather like a book I once read. A little boy had been kidnapped and his grandfather was in terrible anguish and worry over the lad. However, when at last the boy was returned to him, the grandfather held back the urge to run to the child and embrace him, as that would only embarrass the lad. Instead the two just shook hands. But, oh, what feeling there was in that clasp of hands.

Such was the silence.

THE DREAM CAME AGAIN that night, harrowing and daunting without mercy or reprieve. It came in a cold, blackened haze that made my fingers and arms sluggish with disuse. The robed figure came again, lunging at me with a long, wretched blade that severed the quilt tucked above my shoulders. I could almost smell the winter's cold, almost feel the wet, heavy snow bite at my face and ears. But it was not until an extra weight loomed over me that I truly awoke.

It was not a dream.

I lashed out feet first, heels shooting upwards through the blankets and catching my attacker's jaw and hurling him backwards into the wall with a comforting thud. I leapt from the quilt's deathly grasp and began searching the side table. God, where was it? My knife. Where—

The door was flung open with a terrific bang.

"Lawrence, what the devil?" My stunned attacker whirled around just as Keane began charging at him with ready fists. He was a split second too slow, or perhaps the stranger was just too fast, for a sturdy hook smashed into Keane's shoulder. My companion did manage to wedge the knife out of his hands and kicked the wicked object across the floor until it skidded to a halt at my bare feet. Where the stranger was strong; however, Keane had the advantage of his height and agility in spite of his years. My mind, now ridded of all sleep and sluggishness, wanted to pounce on the robed man and tear him away from my companion as the two swung their battalion of fists and knees. In a mighty shove, Keane hurled the man to the other side of the room and prepared to fight further when, without the slightest hesitation, the man leapt out the window and was immediately swallowed by the darkness. In the brief, horrid moment when I caught a glimpse of the stranger's face just before he sprang out into the cold, I found I saw no face, but a black mask which seemed to be sewn into the hood of his robe. I edged to the window, peeked out at the emptiness, and shoved the frame down with both hands.

I turned to Keane then, who was bent over with his hands propped on his knees and sucking in sharp breaths of cold air. A bit of snow had blown through the window and matted itself into his hair and pajama shirt. After a moment he pushed himself upward and gingerly rolled his shoulder he had been bashed into the wall.

"I have heard of Ankou visiting people's homes in the night, but I had hoped I had a few years yet before seeing him." Keane chuckled at his own wit, a soft, dry sound which was cut short with a hiss as a hand found its way to his ribs. "Bloody hell." I slipped from the room and returned with a half drunk bottle of Jameson, which seemed to have entered my life frequently in the past month. I poured Keane a glass of the pale liquor, then water for myself, before sitting on the bed beside him. He threw back a gulp of his drink, swallowed, and cradled the glass between his hands. I watched the gears of his mind turn and pulse, greased by the alcohol and cigarettes, which soon made an appearance. Within the tobacco haze his eyes pierced the dimness of the room.

After a long while, and well into his second drink, his focus shifted from the wall to his dry, thin hands etched with scars and old injuries.

"I think," He cleared his throat. "I think it would be best if you didn't sleep in here anymore. You take the sofa tonight and I'll—"

"Keane, you absolutely cannot spend the rest of the night in that grumpy old armchair. You'll end up with a crick in your back and I'll never hear the end of it." My protest was, at best, futile, but it was a courageous attempt all the same. On most any occasion, with most anyone other than this man, I might have expected him to take me up on this offer, or laugh at the thought of a woman turning away such a show of masculinity. Keane; however, had always been the ideal gentleman. His thin lips curled at the edges.

"I assure you I will survive. Now, bring the pillow and quilt with you." Keane rose, brushed away a bit of ash from the knees of his pajamas, and left the room, though he did not allow the door to shut behind him. I carried the necessities to the sitting room; however, rather than making my place on the sofa, I folded the quilt in half like a sleeping bag in front of the fire. Keane, ever the gentleman, began to sputter, but I held my ground and stretched myself before the final glow of the embers. At last he chuckled, threw up his hands, and settled himself on the sofa with his fingers entwined behind his head.

As the final tails of smoke wagged upward into vanishing streams, I found myself staring at the top of Keane's head resting on the arm of the sofa with his feet propped up on the other end. Another quilt covered most of his legs and fell just above the wooden floor. The soft rise and fall of his chest, the almost art-like stillness to his features, forced me to believe he had again fallen asleep. Often in such times he looked like some acrylic scene torn from a painting as the grey wisps of night caused many of the lines etched into his face fade into near oblivion. The blond tint to his hair slowly darkened until it overpowered the grey. To watch him had always been such a peaceable thing, but oh how I started when, though quiet, a rich, deep voice came to me over the final breaths of the greying embers.

"Lawrence, are you ... are you in love with Michael?" Those words, the fated question which struck my ears and made them ring like gunfire.

"What?"

"Do you l—"

"I heard the question, I just never thought I would ever hear such a thing from you. Didn't you tell me once 'romance is what people do when they have nothing better to fulfill their time'?" I noted the subtle shift of Keane's shoulders as his hands slipped from behind his head.

"I don't believe I said it with quite so much distaste. Adoration—romance—can be a wonderful thing if it is shared with the right person, though I don't believe one should throw away their bachelor life simply because they want to spend their life with someone. The only reason to give up such a life of immense freedoms is because you wouldn't want to live *without* them." Keane cleared his throat, a thick, damnably frustrating sound. "But you have not answered my question." I sighed. It is one thing to be asked such a question, and quite another when the person to whom you must answer is the very man you have known for the better portion of a decade. But he had asked. Worse, he was now waiting patiently with his eyes enamored by the pattern of his fingers clasped together. I opened my mouth, shut it, and opened it again. To my eternal shock, words began to come.

"I suppose I haven't answered your question; because, I don't know *how*. I don't know how I'm supposed to feel." Keane's head shot up and he whirled himself around until he was facing me entirely.

"Supposed to feel? Lawrence, you are never *supposed* to feel anything. Feelings between men and women—boys and girls—are so fragile, almost like butterflies. If you try to feel—try to feel what you think you should—you will miss some of the most wonderful moments life has to offer."

"But knowledge and intellect—"

"—Are both fine and important things, but I have found even subdued emotions can sharpen the mind in ways unimaginable by cold scientists. Your Benjimin Franklin was well known for his time with the women of Paris, and even Einstein married twice." I grinned impishly.

"Keane, are you suggesting great minds are also cads and playboys?" My companion laughed, a sharp but warm ringing which brought the image of sailing ships and sails snapping gayly at the wind's hand.

"I may be old, Lawrence, but I am hardly a prude. Life is a wonderous thing, and one should live it for the moment, while still ready to improve one's mind as if time was of no importance." Keane laid back again and allowed his eyelids to fall halfway over those stormy, blue oceans.

"I won't press you for an answer about Michael tonight. But I do expect one . . . later."

CHAPTER THIRTY-THREE

The following morning I awoke to find the snow had at last ceased its harrowing plight to puffs no more fierce than a cloud of Keane's tobacco smoke. The reprieve would not last. The clouds foretold as much, and yet the brief spark of freedom was cooled by the enormous, white monsters that stood to Keane's knees as he waded through their evil murk.

"There's no doubt about it." He shouted to me. "We're snowed in. Town must be fifteen to twenty miles from here." I folded my arms and leaned against the door frame.

"And even if we could get through we might only get a few miles before it starts snowing again. Then where would we be?"

"Where indeed." Keane fought his way back to the house where he began brushing the snow from his long legs. Large chunks of white splattered to the floor in future puddles as he toed off his shoes.

We carefully danced around the night's adventure, and most certainly conversation, but it hung in the air in a thick stream of smoke. So thick was it, I found it difficult to see Keane clearly through the dismal haze. Who was this man who asked such a daunting question. Surely there must be some logical explanation hidden beneath his motives. Surely I knew him better than this shadow in the grey. He certainly knew me.

Damn it, of course I knew him.

He was Brendan Keane, professor of psychology. He had been born here in County Cork in 1893. He was a few inches of six feet with striking blue eyes, greying-blonde hair, and the build of a guard.

Name, rank, and serial number.

Keane, who was all these things I mentioned, also was a million things more. He was a brother, an uncle, a man retired from the navy. And yet, as I watched him rid himself of winter's wet and stride toward the fireplace, I knew I had missed some great trait gaping idiotically at me. He was a gentleman. And it was as this gentleman—this epitome of all gentleman—I found him to be one of the most infuriating persons with whom I had ever found friendship.

Friendship. Now there's a word. It sounds entirely pathetic when rolling off of one's tongue and only finds its true meaning when it would be rude to say a person was merely an acquaintance. But with Keane it was true.

He sat back in the armchair, propped his feet up on a stool near the fire, and began sifting through a stack of newspapers several weeks old and thoroughly stained and smudged. Even with news he had most likely already heard in the Duck, Keane made it a point to scoff loudly and stab a finger into each offending headline.

"Lawrence, what is the world coming to? Moral discrepancy. Government corruption. Violence. Scandal. It's appalling."

"Says the man who fought in the first world war, returned to fight in the cause of Irish independence, and throws himself headlong into a brutal case involving a murderer who has decided to clean the world however he likes." Keane set aside the tattered papers.

"Ah, I was hoping we could discuss last night before Bridget finishes making breakfast. I take it that was the same robed man you mentioned before?"

"It really is difficult to tell."

"But you think it was."

"It seems logical." Keane nodded slowly, a long motion propelling his chin almost to the open collar of his shirt.

"So it does. Now then, if that is the case, and if our theory is correct on his motives, why—"

"—the hell would he go after me?" My companion grunted some sort of agreement and began tugging incessantly on his left ear. "Keane, I hardly know who this man is, let alone what he thinks of me. For all I know he might think I am an old girl of his who tried to bed two men without losing the other." I did manage a brief jolt of laughter from Keane with this comment, but it didn't last. The harsh noise dissipated into the rafters, along with any amusement dancing in his eyes. It was never safe to look into those eyes. They pulled words from your mouth you would rather have not said and compelled you to the truth, no matter how long you had meticulously created the perfect lie.

Keane, who had already removed his feet from the stool, positioned himself that he was sitting on the arm of the armchair, rather than in it. With him sitting in such a way. We were level, eye to eye, mind to mind, yet I found myself at a dreadful disadvantage.

"Lawrence, you must promise me you will not leave this house without myself or Sean at any time of the day."

"Why on earth would I go outside? Look, it's already beginning to snow harder again. Besides, I have always been perfectly capable of taking care of myself. I am hardly a babe in the woods."

"Be that as it may—"

"Really, Keane, to do such a thing would be an insult to my entire sex. To need a man for protection is becoming as outdated as the idea women are too inept to vote. Men and women are, though different, equals in their own distinct ways."

"Indeed?" He ventured sarcastically. He knew very well where I stood on such matters, and through the years I too had become increasingly aware of his agreement to such advancements in women's position in the world.

Keane's eyes searched mind for the better part of eternity before he rapped his hand on the side of the armchair, harrumphed, and gave a quick, exasperated slap to the newspapers beside him.

"Very well, Lawrence, I take your point, but at least promise me you will be extra cautious. No unnecessary risks."

"No taking candy from strangers, you mean? Relax, Keane, I was only jesting. You would think I was five years old. Fine, I promise. You really do worry too much. It isn't good for you." My companion's shoulders stiffened, then instantly slackened again, as if such comments were not worth the energy. I even caught the slight rumble of laughter.

"'*The true militant suffragette is an epitome of the determination of women to possesses their own souls.*'"

"Emily Davison, 1913, just before she was trampled to death, though I think I prefer Christabel Pankherst. '*Remember the dignity of your womanhood. Do not appeal, do not beg, do not grovel. Take courage, join hands, stand besides us, fight with us.*'"

"Lines well said for a time when such phrases of '*take courage*' or '*fight with us*' were used for the men." I looked at Keane, seemingly for the first time that morning, and sat down on the edge of the sofa with only a few feet of floor between us.

"They were words which needed to be said, for both men and women. Without change, what can we do but die?"

"But, without a life well lived, for what would death be valued?"

"And what is it you two are doing talking about sad things so early in the morning?" Bridget appeared from nowhere with a pink and white floral apron tied about her waist and her brown hair curling to her shoulders. "Only fat old men and creaky spinster women have time for such talk, so. I made eggs, rashers, and some of those scones you like so much, Bren." You would have to be blind not to see how Keane's eyes lit up. "Sean will be coming in for breakfast soon enough—had to go see a man about a wee dog, so he did—but there's no reason for you both not to start at it before it gets cold."

MRS. MCCARTHY WOULD kill me, murder me in cold blood with her rolling pin. But Bridget Fiona Keane, sister of Brendan Keane, and wife of her own doctor, could cook. And exceptionally well. The eggs and rashers had been fried evenly on both sides, something at which Mrs. McCarthy too excelled. The scones; however, were not like Keane's those prize-winning treats made by his housekeeper. These were not only light and flakey, but almost buttery beneath the thick globs of cream and jam. I watched with no end of amusement as Keane ignored the first two staples of breakfast and dove for the scrumptious pile stacked neatly in the middle of the table.

"Marvelous." Keane praised. "Absolutely marvelous." I pushed the plate of scones toward my companion, while tugging the rashers a bit more in my direction. Bridget began pouring the tea.

"I'm glad you like them, so. That's what I said to meself, anyroad. 'Bridget,' I said. 'Sure, wouldn't it be grand if you made those scones Bren likes so much. He'd be so much happier for it, so he would.'"

"And indeed I am." Keane reached out and patted his sister's hand, causing her smile to widen as a child who had just been commended by their father. Though it wasn't far from the truth. Keane had never been libral with the presentation of such sentimental accolades, but it did not so much to disappoint as it did to make his praises all the more valuable. Bridget nearly toppled over with joy.

"Sure, and that's what I thought. I'd rather you be happy than that grumpy old man you used to pretend to be. Remember that, Bren? Remember the time you said some wicked things to Alice? Shee fairly cried from them, so. Do you remember, Bren?" Keane's eyes dimmed slightly and his lips pursed into a firm line.

"Indeed I do. But in my own defense, she was none too kind in her criticisms of my new suit." Bridget giggled girlishly.

"Sure, she said it made ya look like one of those dandies. Oh, wasn't she one for the gab." Suddenly Keane's sister stood straight as an arrow looked him straight in the eyes. "Would you like to see her? Sure, she's gotten on in years, but she's still got the wit of a jackrabbit in the briar."

"It would be an honor." Bridget fairly skipped away as Keane began folding his napkin onto the table. His eyes were so entirely engrossed with the action I had not the chance to ask who this Alice was before his sister again returned, walking with a gait so painfully slow one might have thought it a royal march and clutching her friend's hand. Keane immediately pushed back his chair and rose to his towering height before reverently shaking the pale hand of the newest arrival.

It was one of the few times I had ever seen Keane shake hands with a rag doll.

Where one of the black button eyes was scarcely hanging to the faded face with a few wisps of thread, the other had been replaced entirely with a brown one, most likely from an old coat. Her smile had become lopsided through the decades, her dress was torn and patched, and only a few strings of yarn hair remained on her head, but her owner revered her more highly than a princess.

Bridget brought Alice to me and I too shook hands with the doll, noting the ink smudges on her fraying arm. When at last the formalities were concluded, we all three—all *four*—sat down once more to breakfast with Alice positioned neatly in her owner's lap. As I reached for the rashers again, Bridget quickly leaned her ear down to the doll's painted lips and immediately sat up again to face her brother.

"Alice says you are looking quite distinguished today." Keane sat a little straighter and his near constant smile grew a bit fuller.

"That is kind of you to say, Alice. Would you care for a scone? They are quite good."

"Oh no!" Bridget exclaimed. "I'm afraid she says she can't today. She is on a slimming diet." I noted the brief speck of amusement flash in Keane's eyes.

"Is she indeed?"

"She says you might need to try it if you keep eating all those scones." It was inevitable. I let out a great bark of laughter.

"I—I'm sorry Keane, but—but really this is too much." Bridget cocked her head at me.

"Alice wants to know what's so funny. Sure, she likes a good joke." I was stuck, and yet suddenly liberated.

"Mrs. McCarthy—Keane's housekeeper—often says the same thing." Now it was Keane who was left gaping at me, but soon he too burst in great guffaws of laughter. It was true, Mrs. McCarthy *did* use such a threat, but not even she could deny Keane was slim while still retaining the peak of masculine figuratures. I did note; however, the soft grumble as he pushed the plate of scones away with a reluctant shove.

"Does Alice have any other suggestions?" Bridget nodded.

"She says you need a shave and—"

"Good Morning." Sean ambled into the room, filling most of the doorframe. His nose and cheeks were bright red from the cold and flecks of white winter dust had lodged themselves into his red hair. In his bright red sweater and black trousers, I swore he could have been Father Christmas two months late for his rounds. When his eyes caught sight of Alice; however, his joviality lessened considerably as he took in the doll well on its way to that great toy chest up in the sky.

"Good morning, Alice. My, you look tired. Didn't you sleep well?" Bridget's back went straight in the wooden chair.

"She said she slept very well."

"But look at those lines under her eyes. She needs more sleep."

"No, she is quite awake."

"But look at her hands. Why, the poor girl's shivering. Bridget, me darling, why don't you wrap her up in something warm from our room and let her have a little rest." The woman's eyes began to collect water at the edges.

"But she doesn't like to sleep alone." Sean thought for a moment, rubbed a few flecks of snow from his chair, and allowed his voice, already gentle though it was, to fall scarcely as rough as a calm sea polished over with glass.

"I have an idea, then. Why don't you go lie with her for a bit until she is feeling her old grad self?" As if a sufficient answer, Bridget bounded off with the little ragdoll clutched in her arms. Sean sighed heavily and sat down at the table.

"Brendan, whatever you thought when buying her that doll, you thought right. She won't let anyone else touch it." Keane grinned and reached for the eggs.

"To be honest, I am still rather shocked she kept it all these years." Or that it lasted this long, I added silently. My companion leaned over his plate, his elbows scarcely avoiding the smudge of jam on the table. "In your professional opinion, how is her condition progressing?" Sean—*Doctor* Sean McCladah—bowed his head toward Keane.

"Professionally, I would say she is improving grandly. She has her moments, as you just saw, but, for the most part, she is doing well. Far better than she could have done in the institution." The tendons in Keane's neck flinched noticeably as his brows furrowed.

"Yes, I visited there a few times. Dreadful place."

"It does serve some purpose for the worse cases, but, for others, it's just a pot to throw the chicken in."

"Or have a libral use of morphine injections. Fortunately I didn't notice any ill effects on Bridget." Sean's eyes lowered to his plate.

"Scars run deep. Men in our profession understand that better than most."

"Indeed." Keane pushed back his chair and brushed a few stray crumbs from his shirt. "Now, if you'll excuse me, I have been informed I am in need of a shave."

"KEANE, STOP LAUGHING. You might slit your throat." My companion brought the razor away from the bits of foam left on his face, but his rumbling chuckle did not cese.

"But what you suggest, my dear Lawrence, is nothing short of lunacy."

"Says the psychiatrist. Now really, I'm serious. Why couldn't it work?"

"If that character of yours—Captain Moore, is it?—Yes, if your captain tried to dive into the ocean to save some men from a shark, he would be killed himself. And then where would your book be?" I huffed dryly.

"With one heck of a plot twist." Keane smiled graciously before again bending his tall frame over the mirror with the deathly razor poised to strike away the morning scruff. It was an artform, completely reserved for the male sex as was pipe tobacco and stout. And Keane was most definitely a man.

I observed his every motion from the washroom door. When the razor retired, the necktie came. Then the waistcoat. Then the jacket. At last he had built himself an empire against the world, only to willingly throw himself into its mighty jaws. Alice, doll though she was, had certainly been correct in one thing.

Keane *was* distinguished.

I stepped aside and followed him to the sitting room, the ever constant scent of cigarette tobacco leading me along. He positioned himself on the sofa, unfolded his reading glasses, and began shuffling through the scraps of paper bearing my penciled script. They were only brief specks of stories—mere snippets—but Keane had always been a man enthralled with the smallest points of literature. He stabbed his finger into the top most scrap as I sat next to him.

"This part is quite good, though I might suggest a few changes. For instance, you wrote your Captain briefly visited Italy. Which city?"

"I was unaware the city made much of a difference." Keane glanced at me over his silver rims.

"Indeed, and is your America simply one place without different cultures and traditions? I think not."

"Where would you suggest then? Rome?"

"An overused idea. See, Lawrence, when a place is used repeatedly in literary practices, it becomes stale to the reader. No, he must visit somewhere like Trieste or Palermo. Palermo, now there's a marvelous place: colorful and exciting. Yes, I would certainly suggest Palermo." Had it been anyone but myself, they would have missed it. If it had been half a decade ago, I would have missed it. I would have missed the slight wistfulness to his English drawl, the nostalgic incline of his syllables until they were filled with the warmth of days past. Then again, had I changed my path of life a decade ago, I would have missed Keane entirely.

CHAPTER THIRTY-FOUR

The snow storm soon took up its blinding shroud and hurled itself down onto our little patch of earth. The winds too returned as screaming banshees, shrieking threats of imminent doom. It did not shake us though, for we were steadfast and—at the risk of sounding sentimental—together. A bee cannot stand alone against the elements, but a hive can endure time itself with the intoxicating bustle of work without thought for death lurking at their door. Such were we. Bridget was often in the kitchen, creating an array of goods from the well-stocked pantry. Alice did make a few more appearances, but they were brief and not quite so thick with criticisms toward Keane. (Though Sean did take the brunt end of a few of her sharper comments.) As for myself, I threw myself entirely into my writing, scratching out idle plots and miscellaneous lines on whatever paper I could lay my hands on: a few shreds of yellow stationary, reips, even the margin of the old newspapers were not safe from my lunacy. Keane would then shuffle through my trove of ink stains with a critical eye. More often than not his views were far from optimistic, yet they were filled with steam, shoving me forward along a safer line of tracks. I had not yet mustered the courage to ask about Palermo, but with every swift brush of his hand along the paper scraps, or deep glimmer at the edge of his eyes, I was reminded of it. There was a wall there, safe and secure, and I could not cross. It had been built recently, but the mortar had dried before I could tear it down. The wall was not a tall one. I could still see Keane just as easily as I had sitting beside him on the fraying sofa, but he was reserved and cautious. When I reached forward for a line sprawled on a month old newspaper, his hand retreated, not drastically, but noticeably. He did not sit directly beside me, but merely on the same sofa. I thought nothing of it. Keane was a man often subjected to short periods of moodiness. It was not until night fell upon us I found myself questioning the extent of his seclusion. He was there with Bridget, the younger man I had not the chance and fortune to meet. He was there as she sat against him with her head resting on his shoulder. He was there with the scones, and Alice, and the stories, and the books he read late into the night.

But with me, he was not but a shadow. And it was not until a few evenings later I realized why.

I had grown accustomed to seeing his long form stretched out on the sofa, his features rewinding the clock as the final glimmers of the fireplace flitted along the air as a warning to approaching darkness. His hands still clenched the book open face down in his lap. He did not snore, but his lips were slightly parted as if waiting for the perfect moment to do so. The light rise and fall of his chest was the only movement in an otherwise still world.

"Keane?" The book slipped to the floor in a woosh of bound pages. The world shook.

"Lawrence? Bloody hell, what time is it?" He jammed the heels of his hands into his eye sockets before sweeping them through his unruly hair.

"I think I have your answer." They were words more powerful than a thousand alarm clocks, for his head shot up and his fell legs down much too close to the book splattered on the floorboards.

"You do." It was not a question. Rather, his groggy state left only the tone one falls to upon accepting a bad tooth. It must be pulled, but to do so would either alleviate the discomfort, or leave one looking like a fool. I propped myself up off the floorboards. My legs ached, my arms burned, and my hands clenched themselves together until the fingers were close on white.

"Keane, I—I don't know how to say it."

"Straight out. That's always the best way."

"I don't love Michael." Keane didn't move, didn't flinch, didn't . . . breathe.

"You don't?"

"No. I like him, but I don't *love* him. I'm sorry." His head jerked upward with a set expression I had learned to know well, and had so terribly missed.

"What the hell are you sorry for? You can't force your feelings, just as you can't force a jackass up a hill."

"I—" My voice stopped and my eyes were suddenly entertained by the book still lying prostrate on the floor. A page had folded beneath it in its tumble, and was no doubt permanently creased. "Keane, why did God make emotions so damn difficult?" He laughed. And why shouldn't he? I sounded like a damn child foolishly pondering the ins and outs of life without the most basic understanding for life itself. It was incredulous, and yet—

WHAM!

The door burst open as a dark figure flew in from the cold. I was not aware of Keane's touch until I was behind him, his right hand almost wrenching my arm from it's socket as it held me back. His fingers dug into my skin for a long, painful moment, but, before I could shout some protest of his ridiculously chivalrous behavior, his voice shot among the rafters in one enormous huff of air.

"Michael, dear boy. How on earth did you get here?" Keane's grasp relaxed and he allowed me to stand beside him, rather than my body being pinned against the edge of the fireplace. Indeed the man *was* Michael, albeit a scruffier, wool-covered version. He smiled and walked—as best as one can in all those warm layers—over to Keane and began pumping his arm with such velocity as one never should a man over thirty-five.

"Half the town is out looking for you, Uncle. After you broke away from Da's party, he thought for sure you'd be lying face down somewhere. And Joanna, thank God you're safe. May I?" I was distinctly aware of two, snow-caked gloves being matted against the side of my head and his cold lips pressed against my cheek. I was also aware of Keane's grasp, which had yet to fully leave my arm, tighten briefly, as if the final tremor of an invisible flinch. His voice, as always, was level and polite to a tea.

"How did you find us?" His nephew stepped back to peel away his mangled scarf.

"Didn't you notice? The snow's stopped again. I have a car waiting up at the top of the hill." As if visible from this distance, Michael glanced at the window. "We better leave now before the snow starts again. The sun should be up soon. Get your things—"

"All in due time." Keane sighed. "Lawrence, start getting ready. Michael, there's some food in the kitchen. I should go say good-bye." The young man turned away just as Keane stepped toward the master bedroom. This time it was I who grabbed his arm.

"Do you want me to come with you?"

"No thank you. I think it would be for the best if she heard it from me. I fear it will be quite a blow."

"We can come back in a few months. You don't have to stay away this time." My companion smiled gently and grasped my hand resting on his arm.

"*'That is my home of: if I have ranged,*
Like him that travels I return again,
Just to the time, not with the time exchanged.'" I smiled.
Shakespeare.

Keane pushed off from me with a final squeeze to my fingers and I, for the first time in a long time, realized how quickly the world was spinning at my feet. How it had changed—how *I* had changed—since last I had looked. But, unlike King Lear, I would not try to command the storm, but throw myself into it with full knowledge of the dangers and trials awaiting me.

As I began stuffing Keane's extra shirt into a canvas bag, I became vaguely aware of a sobbing seeping through the walls. Though not melodious, it was heart wrenching with high, quivering wails of hopelessness, which were gradually quelled by a rhythm of words tied together in consoling phrases. To me they were muffled, but, when Keane reappeared at the door, I would have been blind not to note the damp spots on his shoulder, the defeated set of his jaw, or the slight trembling of his hands before he shoved them into his gloves. We were off.

WHILE THE SNOW MIGHT have stopped upon Michael's arrival, it returned full force a few miles into our journey. Where the snow piled well past Keane's knees, it almost swallowed my legs completely. The frozen white worked its way through my layers and against my skin. When we reached the foot of the hill, it was impossible to see much more than a few hundred yards past our noses. Keane squinted upward through the blinding sheets, dubiously eyeing the steep incline. For a instant, I wondered if he was questioning whether I could manage such a climb, or if his own limbs would stand the rigor. I knew it to be the first when he glanced at me. Or, more specifically, the nape of my neck where the bump had been. As if reassurance I was not about to topple at his feet, I began heaving my layered form up the hill.

Halfway up my lungs were on fire, threatening to burst if I dared another step. Keane too seemed to be suffering the same effects, but he pressed on after Michael. If I fell so much as a step behind, his hand was immediately on my arm; not so much for necessary assistance as a silent voice urging me onward. If the sun was near to an appearance, it was impossible to tell. The billowing snow created a darkness even the infamous sun could never penetrate.

May you see God's light on the path ahead
When the road you walk is dark . . .

A thousand ghosts wailed at our ears, beckoning us toward death's cold hand. Such noise was almost enough to make one wish for such a fate, but how many had the storm already swallowed in its jaws? How many families grieved for the prey of these howling wolves?

. . . May you always hear,
Even in your hour of sorrow,
The gentle singing of the lark . . .

Again I felt Keane's hand, but this time it came to my back and tugged me closer to him, rather than merely pushing me onward.

. . . When times are hard may hardness
Never turn your heart to stone . . .

His tall frame shielded me from only a miniscule portion of the thrashing snow, but it was enough to make me seal the gap between us until my arm was securely around his waist, and his my shoulder. Michael had long since faded into the shadows before us. Yet, no fear had I as I caught the hesitant whiff of cigarette tobacco battling the storm as it absorbed every inch of my companion's clothing. Many of the more conservative class deemed it an evil habit, along with drinking and a few hands of well dealt cards at the table. To me, it was the sweetest of all worldly reminders.

. . . May you always remember
when the shadows fall –
You do not walk alone.

At last, we staggered up the last few steps to the top, the great huffs of Keane's breath only matched by my own. I bowed down and began gulping great mouthfuls of frost-bitten air into my lungs until my vision cleared from long, shaggy blurs. It was flat here. Flat, frozen land spotted by the few visible tops of trees and perhaps a dozen jagged stones. The stone circle. My soul rejoiced in such feet and I could very well feel my heart leap and bash against my ribcage.

We had done it! We were safe!

Safe.

Such a magnificent, positively marvelous word. I turned to Keane. Safe, I thought, we were safe. The stone circle was not far from Thomas' home. Only a few miles, which would be made a thousand times easier by the use of Michael's car.

Safe, my head sang.

Safe.

And then I saw Keane's face.

It was not of a man rejoicing, nor even a man struck with the relief and hope of living to see another day. It was shock. I thought he was having a heart attack. Honest, I did. It is a horrid thought considering he was a man in his fifties (though he could pass for a man a decade younger), but his expression was so horribly contorted and his jaw so stubbornly set, it was in fear I followed his gaze toward our more immediate surroundings. All was white spotted with variations of the most dismal grey. It was a picture show at the cinema. Not so much as a speck of color dotted the next few hundred yards.

I could not see the road.

I could not see a car.

I did; however, see the barrel of a gun poised directly at Keane's chest.

CHAPTER THIRTY-FIVE

"I thought you would have been smarter than this, Uncle. Everyone else thinks you are a scholar."

Keane straightened his long body slowly, looking terribly, utterly exhausted. His eyes seemed to immediately glaze over, but not from his heated temperament, but something I had seen only when he spoke of Bridget. When at last his voice came, it was as flat as death and twice as lifeless.

"By God, Michael, put that thing down." Keane's nephew cackled and steadied his hands more firmly on the black monster leering at my companion's lepels.

"Are you blind? Do you think I would take all the effort of bringing you up here only to release you into the world?" His wicked laugh shot out again and I was hit, pierced to the core of my being. Keane did not fare much better. I could almost imagine his blood pouring outward from a gaping hole in his heart. Dark, metallic blood; the only color in an otherwise colorless scene.

"You wouldn't use that." Keane reasoned evenly. "Not after the war. Not after the others." I stood bewildered. Had Keane seen Michael during the war? Others . . . ?

Michael grinned, a flash of fangs.

"Surprise, surprise, Joanna. I must say, you said many fine things about my Uncle's mind, though I believe he forgot shell-shock can be treated. The flinch took a bit longer to cure, but it too disappeared with time. It's just a shame you both won't live long enough to better learn how."

"Why kill us?" I ventured. "Why kill those women and the boy? Surely they could not have hurt you" The young man—the murderer—relaxed slightly, but the revolver did not.

"Joanna, as a writer I thought you would know better than anyone. Society is nothing more than a slum, a great big bawdy house of human dirt. Do you know where we are? The altar of the Druids. You know, I think they were right in many respects, especially their ideas in wiping out the evil. Eileen O'Brian was a thief. Agatha Brown and Joan Kelly were whores. Prostitutes."

"And Curran?" Keane shot. The grin on Michael's face only broadened into a snarl.

"Was that the lad's name? He was nothing. A speck of dust—"

"A *child*. Little more than a boy."

"And if I had let him grow to a man what would he have been? A thief? A cad? A drunkard? A lunatic?" Keane's teeth clenched back a thousand words. With wrenching effort, I stretched my hands open before me and studied the thin creases along each knuckle.

"Why us, then?" I asked. "What immoral acts have we committed?" The gun barrel shifted toward me, lowering slightly from Keane's height.

"*We*?" Michael said delightedly. "I almost forgot how attached you are to the old man. Though I suppose I shouldn't be surprised. I found you out, Joanna. I knew from the moment you punched me for kissing you. It was sealed when I found you this morning."

"What was sealed?" Keane barked, trying chivalrously to tempt the weapon's aim from my coat front. His nephew didn't budge.

"I should have seen it sooner in her irrational fondness for you, Uncle. She's your fallen woman, your slut—"

The gun shot exploded at the same instat Keane's body lunged forward, the bullet piercing hundreds of snowflakes as my companion's body tumbled face down into a drift.

Face down. My mind screamed. *Face down and not to awaken. Face down. God, Lawrence, do something.*

When I started for him; however, the silver muscle swung wildly back to me.

"Tsk, tsk, Joanna. Stay back from him. Good lass. It has never been healthy for a man to stand up for a streetwalker." Keane pushed himself up from the ground and squared his shoulders.

"I'm alright, Lawrence. Seems Michael here isn't as fine a shot as he would like."

"Oh, I'm an excellent shot." The young man cooed. "But I'm not about to let an old goat like you deprive me of the satisfaction of victory. Oh no, dear, *dear* Uncle. No, you shall get to watch Joanna die of a slow—and I assure you, excruciating—procedure. Then you can endure the same."

"You have no right to kill her." Keane protested icily. "She is a perfectly respectable young woman. Besides, you aren't wearing your black robe." It was superfluous, the garment. I knew that all too well. It was as much for self satisfaction than true show.

"The robe? That isn't important. The Druids were a good and noble sort. They purged the earth of your scum and sinfulness. I was only paying homage to him. Surely, Uncle, you know of theatrical endings."

"I do, but if you are so willing to use a revolver now, why not use it on Joan Kelly? Wasn't that a bit much?" Michael grimaced.

"Ah, my one falt. She pulled the gun on me and beat me to the chase. Lucky the thing didn't fire for her. It made it all the easier until the damn woman fell." Suddenly the young man cackled as though he had recited an ancient joke, rather than the terms of a woman's death. "A fitting end, really." My stomach lurched. How had I been so wrong? Upon our first meeting, I had thought Michael a man no less than a man. He was a successful student, climbing the ladder of cultures both past and present. I had thought, of all people, he had been sane. A bit eccentric, perhaps, but sane.

But the fields of eccentricity had long since overgrown with sheer madness.

It was demencia, pure and simple. Where St. Patrick had succeeded in driving the Druids from Ireland, he had not been able to remove their blasphemous stain from time's course shroud. The black seed had been sewed in this young man's mind and strangled all reason and logic.

A nightmare of a thousand figures in dark robes marched around us, wickedly leering through the spitfire of snow and ice. Their faces were gone. Their heads nonexistent save expressionless skulls with jaws hung down loosely. Their eye sockets were not but hollow spaces between the grey bone. The black fabric draped over their rotting bones were held shut by a single cord, and the long, stiff tail ends slicked against their fleshless legs. It bore the same distinct tick of a clock, cackling with the second and laughing as each minute slipped away. A minute closer to the gun. A minute closer to death. Their feet—or where the such parts should have been—left no markings in the snow save a black liquid which grew and swelled with every step, crawling toward me through the snow. It grabbed my ankles, pulling me downward with singing fingers.

To Hell.

The hissed.

To Hell and bered of this world.

And then they too vanished into the snow, leaving me with the sickening twist of my stomach and a numbness which had settled between my ears long before. Ice too had begun to form in the hollow, freezing all knowledge of my surroundings before Keane's voice came as a glob of spit in the snow.

"Michael, I'll make you a proposition."

"Proposition?" The young man seemed far from convinced. Rather, his cold, green eyes snapped with amusement.

"You can do what you wish with me. I'm certainly not getting any younger. My life has been one well lived, and I could die now without regret. But Lawrence has not seen enough of her own life yet. She still has time to marry and settle down if she wishes to do so. Would it be fair for you to take her now before she is even thirty? If you give me your word that you will not so much as touch Lawrence, I will even write a suicide note. It will ruin my name, and you will have your victory." He was serious, the flint grey in his eyes proved it.

"Keane, you can't!" I cried, appalled.

"Do I have your word?" He repeated coldly. Never had I thought to see Keane a desperate man, but he was snatching at mere threads, wisps of ideas that ended in his dishonorable death in either case. Michael; however, seemed to be truly considering the proposition. Keane tried to press the balance.

"You can take it back to my brother and say you found my body and the note in my pocket. Lawrence will go back to England—or America, if she wishes—and you will never see her again."

"You will sign it?" The young man appeared genuinely intrigued.

"If you give me your word." A flash of fangs was all the smile Keane needed. "Lawrence, give me your pen."

"Keane, for God's sake—"

"The pen, Lawrence."

"But—"

"The pen." I stared at Keane, who looked back at me calmly with his hand outstretched. He had removed his glove, exposing a palm crossed with lines and wrinkles. Though I could not see them from a distance, I knew there to be a few small scars etched along the small of his thumb. His forefinger twitched a little in expectation for the writing instrument.

My hand gradually slid into my pocket, finding the cold metal of the pen, and pulled it from my pocket while brushing against the cold sliver of my knife.

"Good." Michael nodded as I cautiously closed the gap to hand Keane the writing tool. My companion met my gaze and allowed his thumb to brush the edge of my palm. The cold, dry skin of his finger met my gloveless hand with a thousand words best left unsaid. It was his eyes that stabbed me. They sealed my mind on the finality of it all. How well I had learned to know those eyes; to read them just as he did his Milton and Behan. What praise I had received in a single glance, or the amusement which erupted from a single flash of blue.

And now it was to be ripped from my grasp. His eyes were to be forever dimmed to the world and all but mine would never again revere him as the man he truly was. It would be a miracle if I myself survived to tell of his selflessness.

"Get on with it." Michael spat impatiently, the gun's sight wavering between us as if unsure who would make the better target. Keane uncapped the pen before again turning his attention to my snow swallowed form.

"Lawrence, I don't seem to have any paper. Do you . . . ?" I checked my pockets and was about to assure him I didn't when my fingers again brushed against my pocket knife. It was not good. Such a small blade would be of no use from this distance, but . . .

Keane's gaze flickered upon my hand, but it was no longer one of hopelessness or apology. By God, it just might—

With a burst of near animal fury, I hurled the metal tool at our attacker's hand with stunning force. The air was again split by an orange flame and the wild scream of flying led. A powerful force lodged into my back and threw me forward into the snow, knocking the wind from my lungs and instead filling them with snow. Keane came up in a crouch and seized my shoulder fiercely.

"Are you hit?"

"Keane, where—?"

"Lawrence, are you alright?"

"Yes, fine. Keane—" Then he was off, scrambling through the snow after the young man who had been prudent, or coward enough, to retreat towards the fleeting outlines of forestry. Before I was fully returned to myself, I found my legs blindly propelling me forward after the vanishing overcoat. In seconds, he too had disappeared completely.

Where Keane's long legs carried him above the white monsters, their wet mouths swallowed well above my furiously pounding knees. The heavy white threatened to wrench away my boots and completely numbed the blocks of ice connected to my ankles.

After an eternity of this lunacy, the wind's deathly howl faltered and calmed, but the snow continued to bombard me in all directions. My eyes stung furiously. My lungs heaved and felt stripped of all oxygen. My limbs screamed of mutiny in the lower ranks. Even my arms, with which I had made my mighty show of strength, felt ripped from my sockets until I was forced to slow my pace. The pit of my stomach cursed our lack of foresight to eat a decent meal before such a journey. I staggered, stumbled, and fell. Then, after clambering upwards, did the same a few hundred yards later. It must have been well over two miles when the sparse trees began to thicken and bow into something resembling forestry. Their snow-laden limbs dipped down toward the ground, groaning with the effort. Through these moaning trees came a resounding crack somewhere in the billowing white; a deep, wet shudder which echoed through the ragged trunks. But there was no missing that definite, hopeless shout, though it be but a whisper through the misery of men.

I ran. Oblivious to the frozen streams and hidden stones clawing at my lower limbs. A hundred times I fell; each time finding it more laborious to struggle back to my feet. Yet I fought on; the drifts holding fast to my legs and releasing them slowly with a deep sucking sound.

At last I came upon a broad clearing where the most sturdy of forests worked diligently to hold the whirling white at bay. There was a stretch of water encircled in these, just as Keane had pointed out early in our visit. Much of the pond was white at the edge, but the center had smoothed into faultless glass.

Apart from a single gaping hole.

I staggered down toward the frozen edge where the head of a dark figure jutted out from where they huddled in a snowbank. My worry gave way in one dull thud.

Relief.

"Keane?" But the shadow didn't turn. Didn't move. Didn't . . . breathe.

I dared a few more steps and salvaged his hat from a pile of snow when at last his shoulders heaved with a single, strained breath.

"I—I tried to warn him. To save him."

"Save him?" I swallowed the remaining space between us in a few balanced strides. His grey-blonde hair was matted to his neck, and where the overcoat had been merely flung aside, his tweed jacket had disappeared completely, along with his tie. All that remained was his shirtsleeves and trousers clinging desperately to his sodden and dripping frame.

With his hat still clutched between my fingers, I reached for his coat, releasing a dry, shaky gasp from its owner. Keane scrubbed tiredly at his face with both hands.

"He made it halfway across before he broke through. I tried to pull him out, but he . . . I even dove in after him. I—I did all I could—" Keane's wavering voice dissipated in a cloud of frozen vapor. I sat beside him and waited patiently as a hunk of snow tumbled from the trees and hit the edge of the pond with a tremendous smack. When Keane's words returned, they came scarcely above a horse whisper.

"My God, Lawrence, he was only a boy. He fought for his country, for his family. To die like that—" I slung the still soggy overcoat over his trembling shoulders, allowing my fingers to linger on the heavy fabric. I shoved aside my immediate instinct to wrap my arms firmly around Keane's shoulders, and instead climbed to my feet, and held my hand down to him.

"As you said, Keane, you did all you could. Come on, let's go home." Come and dry off.

Come and get warm.
Come away.

EPILOGUE

CHAPTER THIRTY-SIX

There is no way to end a story such as this. Keane and I stayed in Ireland until three days after the funeral. Normalcy did not appear immediately upon our return to England, but life did gradually continue onward, as time is always apt to do. The Big Snow of 1947 was later to become one of the most famous winters in Ireland, bringing the untimely end of thousands. A month after Keane and I had again settled—albeit stiffly—into our English lives, he received news his brother, Thomas Francis Keane, had died of a heart attack and Catherine had gone to live with her spinster sister. Keane's old world was quickly crumbling into oblivion with only a few tepid memories of those halcyon days. He carried it well, I thought, and with a dignity I had learned so long ago to expect. It did not eat at him, nor did he wallow in a depressive pit. He had come to terms with his past and it seemed he was ready to paddle forward into the lakes of tomorrow.

We did keep our promise and returned to Ireland a few months later, when at last spring again righted itself in the world. As Keane merrily drove I committed every bit to memory; the rows of trees dancing in the warm breeze, the ocean's gentle song as it lapped against the sandy shores, the vast stretches of various greens, and the stone cottage itself with a beautiful bed of roses bowing as we reached the door. No sooner had Keane stepped upon the doorstep as she was in his arms, her head pressed into his shoulder as he laughed. It was his laugh again, a deep, warm, welcoming noise which made his shoulders shake and the ocean's applause.

That night, when Sean had gone into town and Bridget had fallen asleep against Keane as he read on the sofa, I moved and sat at his other side. At the instant I did so, he pinched the book over his forefinger, closed his eyes, and stretched his legs under a newly purchased coffee table.

"Keane?"

"Hm?"

"You never did tell me what was in the letter Thomas sent you the first time we came." A single eye opened.

"Didn't I?"

"No." Keane laid the book on the table and, careful not to knock Bridget's head from his shoulder, he brought a wrinkled and creased envelope from inside his jacket pocket and dropped it in my lap.

Dear Brendan,

You should come down for a visit soon. It has been too long, and neither of us are getting any younger. My heart's not what it used to be and travel isn't an option. I urge you to come as soon as you can. We are brothers, after all.

Thomas

I HANDED THE LETTER back to Keane.

"That's all?" He slipped it back into his jacket pocket and patted it sentimentally.

"That's all." I sank into the sofa, allowing my shoulder to meet the tweed of Keane's suit. He took up his book again. For a long while there was nothing but the soft echo of thought between us, but there was a warmth to it I had longed to feel for so very long. At last normalcy had again begun to seep into our lives.

And yet . . .

"Keane, we never really discussed how all this ended. Will you—that is—are you alright?" A heavy sigh shook his chest, and I realized my fatal mistake; his cigarettes were out of reach. I rose to get them from the table when I was suddenly aware of his hand gently grasping mine and urging me to sit down again.

"Lawrence, are you familiar with J. M. Barrie?" As he asked he turned over his book so I might see the cover. Again it was not his normal preference. Indeed not, it was *Peter Pan*. I shouldn't have been surprised. He had been reading it aloud to Bridget before she nodded off, so it was only logical he continued on alone. And yet I could not keep a smile from my face at the sight of the childhood story.

"You mean, '*Second star to the right and straight on til morning*'?" Keane chuckled, causing his younger sister to stur slightly.

"Yes. Genius, isn't it? Though I had set my mind on another quotation. '*Never say goodbye because goodbye means going away and going away means forgetting.*' You see, Lawrence, neither you or I will ever forget what has happened here. The human mind just doesn't work to our convenience. We will forever question our actions as a string of 'what if's', but, so long as we never try to do away with who we are, we will always have our memories, both good and painful. They will be a part of us until we die." I stared at the floor.

"That doesn't sound terribly optimistic."

"Ah, but you forget, '*To die will be an awfully big adventure.*'" More Barrie? Damn the man. I laughed.

"Ever the philosopher, eh, Keane?" My companion chuckled, which soon became a long yawn. He gently laid Bridget down on the sofa and stretched his back.

"Go to bed, Lawrence. It's late." I shook my head.

"We've had the argument before. You are *not* sleeping in an armchair." Keane stepped toward me, but I halted him with a raised palm. "No, Keane, you will not win this time with some form of gallantry. My hands shall remain decidedly un-kissed because *I* will be sleeping in the armchair tonight." My companion looked at me with an almost ludicrous amount of shock.

"Win by gallantry. You wound me to even think I would stoop to such depths. I promise I shall not so much as touch your hands."

"And you won't try to trick me with your words?"

"Heavens no, Lawrence. You are far too intelligent." I grinned.

"Very well then, you may do your worst, but I assure you I will not allow you to injure your back by spending the night in some ungodly position." Keane did indeed do his worst. His hands clapped down on my shoulders and I was hardly aware of what he had done until he was well on his way to the armchair.

Damn the man.

Don't miss out!

Visit the website below and you can sign up to receive emails whenever Elyse Lortz publishes a new book. There's no charge and no obligation.

https://books2read.com/r/B-A-DSUO-JLVOB

BOOKS 2 READ

Connecting independent readers to independent writers.

Also by Elyse Lortz

Lawrence and Keane
Come Away
The Crimson Shaw

Poetry for the Wandering Mind
This Midnight Hour

CPSIA information can be obtained
at www.ICGtesting.com
Printed in the USA
BVHW032136131021
618937BV00014B/78